Jane Allen

I LOST MY GIRLISH LAUGHTER

Silvia Schulman Lardner (1913–1993) was born in New York City, the child of Russian Jewish immigrants. She left Hunter College for a job at RKO Studios and later worked for MGM and Selznick International as producer David O. Selznick's personal secretary. In 1935, she cowrote a play with fellow Selznick staffer Barbara Keon, and she worked on *A Star Is Born* (1937) and preproduction for *Gone with the Wind* (1939). She married Ring Lardner Jr. in 1937, quit her job, and began writing *I Lost My Girlish Laughter*, a fictionalized memoir of her years with Selznick. In 1938, she published her novel in collaboration with Jane Shore under the pseudonym Jane Allen. After divorcing Lardner in 1945, she raised their two children and worked for many years as an interior designer and building contractor in California. She died of cancer.

Jane Shore came to Hollywood from New York City in 1928 to write a film for Nancy Carroll, which was ultimately not produced. She collaborated with Silvia Schulman on *I Lost My Girlish Laughter* and continued to write under the pseudonym of Jane Allen for "A Girl's Best Friend Is Wall Street" (adapted for the screen in 1941 as *She Knew All the Answers*). Her novel, *Thanks God! I'll Take It from Here* (1946), written in collaboration with May Livingstone, was later adapted for the screen and retitled *Without Reservations* (RKO, 1946).

J. E. Smyth is a professor of History at the University of Warwick (UK) and the author of several books about Hollywood, including *Nobody's Girl Friday: The Women Who Ran Hollywood* (2018).

I LOST MY
GIRLISH
LAUGHTER

I LOST MY GIRLISH LAUGHTER

Jane Allen

(Silvia Schulman and Jane Shore)

INTRODUCTION BY J. E. SMYTH

VINTAGE BOOKS

A DIVISION OF PENGUIN RANDOM HOUSE LLC

NEW YORK

MELROSE PUBLIC LIBRARY
MELROSE, MASS.

FIRST VINTAGE BOOKS EDITION, NOVEMBER 2019

Introduction copyright © 2019 by J. E. Smyth

Published in the United States by Vintage Books, a division of
Penguin Random House, New York, and distributed in
Canada by Penguin Random House Canada Limited, Toronto.
Originally published by Random House, a division of
Penguin Random House LLC, in 1938.

Vintage and colophon are registered
trademarks of Penguin Random House LLC.

The Library of Congress Cataloging-in-Publication Data
Name: Allen, Jane, pseud.
Title: I lost my girlish laughter / by Jane Allen.
Description: New York : Random House, 1938.
Identifiers: LCCN 38027404
Classification: LCC PZ3.A4271 I
LC record available at https://lccn.loc.gov/38027404

Vintage Books Trade Paperback ISBN: 978-1-9848-9776-3
eBook ISBN: 978-1-9848-9777-0

Author photograph, page 193, courtesy of Ann Waswo and David Lardner
Book design by Christopher M. Zucker

www.vintagebooks.com

Printed in the United States of America
10 9 8 7 6 5 4 3 2 1

To

J. P.
*To remind him that Boy still
meets Girl, and anyway it's a good
paying business*

Contents

Introduction

In early 1937, when film producer David O. Selznick was putting the finishing touches on his classic Hollywood Cinderella story *A Star Is Born*, his former secretary was writing her own version of the film business. The result, *I Lost My Girlish Laughter*, is the most important Hollywood novel that most people have never read.

Though Selznick's place in popular memory has endured thanks to the continued popularity—and notoriety—of his production *Gone with the Wind* (1939), Silvia Schulman is a footnote in Hollywood history—even among mavens and cinephiles. But without Schulman, Selznick arguably would not have bought Margaret Mitchell's novel *Gone with the Wind* or acquired his respectable reputation as an innovative producer of women's pictures. In 1936, Schulman read Mitchell's hefty galleys and, along with her friend and colleague, Selznick's New York–based story editor Kay Brown, badgered the producer to purchase the screen rights for $50,000. Schulman had worked in the film business since the early 1930s, when she left Hunter College for RKO Pictures. She later joined Selznick's MGM production team as his personal secretary and moved with him when he formed his own company in 1935.

Schulman was one of thousands of women who worked for the American film industry in the 1930s. Industry leaders and journalists of the time claimed women made up nearly half of all studio employees and argued that Hollywood was one of the few places where women could earn as much money as men. Actresses such as Carole Lombard, Constance Bennett, and Katharine Hepburn netted salaries higher than President Roosevelt. The public fascination with the lives of Hollywood stars dominated the pages of fan magazines such as *Photoplay* and *Modern Screen*, fueling a popular literary and film genre focused on the highs and lows of "making it" in Hollywood. Most of these stories, perhaps predictably, were about the lives and loves of stars, not secretaries like Miss Schulman, nor the legions of female writers, directors, editors, designers, researchers, agents, journalists, and producers who made their living at the studios. In Selznick's *A Star Is Born*, for example, film-struck aspiring actress Esther Blodgett (Janet Gaynor) heads west to Hollywood, and with the help of a glamorous, self-destructive legend (Fredric March) and a paternal producer (Adolphe Menjou), transforms into star sensation Vicki Lester.

Selznick saw a lot of himself in fictional producer Oliver Niles, the Hollywood grandee who shepherds the starlet to fame. Played by Menjou, Niles was considerate and discreet, a man of impeccable taste—certainly not the Hollywood mogul #MeToo advocates love to hate these days. Oliver Niles would never be caught pinching any secretary's behind. Selznick did care about helping women's careers. His production *What Price Hollywood?* (1932) was part tribute to silent star Clara Bow's struggles with fame; he gave Janet Gaynor a job when Twentieth Century Fox chief Darryl F. Zanuck fired her for growing out of her girlish screen image; he worked with female screenwriters, including Jane Murfin, Sarah Y. Mason, and Wanda Tuchock; and he launched Hepburn's career.

But Silvia Schulman had a different perspective on her boss. Selznick may have liked working with women, but not always in the best way. His clumsy romantic passes, pats, and lunges at female employees were a normal part of the workday in his organization. Early on in her job Schulman had dodged his wandering hands, but she subsequently managed to maintain a respectful working relationship with her boss. Other colleagues willingly said yes to Mr. Selznick.

Like many secretaries, Schulman had a sharp gift for satire honed over many hectic years in the business. She knew where all the bodies were buried—or bedded. But rather unusually, she was also a gifted writer. In 1935, she and friend Barbara Keon cowrote a play with the cheeky polygamous title *Adam Had Three Eves*. Although her boss liked it enough to buy it, Selznick never went forward with the film version. Schulman was not promoted to screenwriter. Instead, the producer kept her busy with dictation and reading "serious" potential properties for production—by *real* writers. Schulman may have fumed, but she wasn't one to waste time. If *Adam Had Three Eves* was just going to be shelved while Selznick took credit for her production advice, Schulman would get even by secretly writing her version of the great American novel. She certainly had enough material, but not much time. As she joked to her friend, the columnist Sheilah Graham, she was "so enamored of her job as confidential secretary" that she worked "sometimes as late as 5:00 a.m." Schulman confided in her boyfriend, publicist and screenwriter hopeful Ring Lardner Jr., but it wasn't until they married and went on their honeymoon in early 1937 that she had time to put everything on paper. The family story goes that they spent their honeymoon in some Laguna Beach hotel *writing*. He worked on a script; she wrote a novel.

At this point, Schulman's former writing partner was too busy to collaborate on a novel; Keon was managing Selznick's stable of male writers in their numerous failed attempts to script *Gone with the Wind*. So Schulman asked another woman with a grudge against the system, Jane Shore, to help shape and polish the manuscript. Shore had come to Hollywood from New York back in 1928, wrote *Broadway Sally* for star Nancy Carroll, and had to watch Fox executives shelve the picture when too many Broadway- and Sally-themed films glutted the new sound-era market. In addition to *Sally's Shoulders* (1928), *Beau Broadway* (1928), and *The Broadway Melody* (1929), Warner Bros. released *Sally* (1929), an adaptation of the classic stage hit, starring Marilyn Miller (the original Broadway Sally). Shore had been out of steady work ever since and had tried joining the new Screen Writers Guild in 1935 in a last-ditch effort to get some decent assignments. The opportunity to help Schulman write a gossipy takedown of Hollywood, and then to sell it for a killing to the very people they were satirizing, was too good to pass up. At night, down at the Lardner-Schulman abode, she helped organize the sequence of stories, gags, and nightmares Schulman had collected from years of working at the top of the picture business.

In a rebuttal of her boss's current rags-to-riches star romance, Schulman gave the secretary's view of the film business in *I Lost My Girlish Laughter*. Like Schulman, protagonist Madge Lawrence is a native New Yorker, an ex–college girl on the lookout for a decent paying job in Hollywood. When a letter of introduction from her newspaper contacts does not open any studio gates, she heads out one evening, depressed and dateless, for a consoling drink or two. It's then that she meets a genial director (likely modeled on Selznick's employee John Cromwell), who, impressed with her college education and the fact she's not just another bleach-blonde on the make, gets her a job as producer Sidney Brand's secretary.

The legendary Brand is, of course, Selznick, who was known for putting his personal "brand" on every aspect of his productions—often to the chagrin of his staff. But readers soon discover that, rather than being one of the young "geniuses of the system," Brand is the comic villain of Madge's story. He's a bumbling, narcissistic hypochondriac with a "flabby mouth and wide, feminine hips" who can't mix his own highballs, holds production meetings in the hospital where his wife is giving birth, and has tantrums when MGM won't loan him Clark Gable (another reference to Selznick's real-life woes over casting *Gone with the Wind*). Told in a series of letters to her girlfriend and aunt (who was based on Schulman's favorite relative, her aunt Ceal Weiss), journal entries, Western Union telegrams, and studio production memos, *I Lost My Girlish Laughter* fuses the perspective of the spunky American girl next door with the insider gossip of Louella Parsons and Sheilah Graham. In the process, Madge gleefully punctures every golden PR myth about Hollywood in circulation. Readers familiar with the so-called greats of the Hollywood novel genre—from Nathanael West's *The Day of the Locust* (1939) to Raymond Chandler's *The Little Sister* (1949)—will feel like they're in new territory with the heroine of *I Lost My Girlish Laughter*. Her free-spirited, first-person narration is reminiscent of the best of P. G. Wodehouse's stories, but there's also something of Edna Ferber's popular workingwoman heroine, Emma McChesney, in Madge Lawrence's down-to-earth charm. And though plenty of Hollywood fairy tales dealt and continue to deal in feminine heartache and betrayal, there's no time for tears or melodrama in this story, as the novel sets up its gags like the best of Leo McCarey's and Frank Capra's screwball comedies. But comparisons and context go only so far: *I Lost My Girlish Laughter* has a style, pace, and content all its own.

Industry bigwigs would later have ulcers just wondering if they were parodied in the text, but Schulman and her cowriter had just as much fun sending up overrated foreign stars such as Marlene Dietrich and Cocoanut Grove snobs like Paulette Goddard. Schulman's hero, the dashing agent Leland Hayward, (recognizably renamed Hayworth Lord in the novel), royally screws Brand over in a contract hire, getting $1,500 a week for an unknown Broadway actor (at the time, $300 would have been the going rate). Friend Kay Brown was renamed Frances Smith, and, as New York story editor, responds to her boss's frantic and illiterate memos with bland efficiency (readers can view some of Selznick's memos, edited for content by Schulman and other studio secretaries, in Rudy Behlmer's classic *Memo from David O. Selznick*, 1972). Another humorous touch was giving a rival MGM producer "Blank" for a surname—presumably because, in real life, Selznick called this rival every imaginable foul word in private. Columnist Louella Parsons became Stella Carsons, or, according to Brand's new high-toned, non-acting foreign star, Sarya Tarn (a version of Dietrich rather than of Samuel Goldwyn's Ukrainian failure, Anna Sten), "that fat peasant." A smart-mouthed if occasionally charming publicity agent, Jim Palmer, was the cover for Schulman's new husband, Ring, who had joined the Selznick empire in 1935 and was immediately smitten, as he wrote to his mother, by "this mad Jewish girl" in the office. Schulman would dedicate the book to him as "J. P." (Jim Palmer) in order to protect his anonymity.

It's been said again and again by historians and journalists that Hollywood during its big bad studio days was strictly a man's world, where women were just decoration for casting couches or secretaries getting the great men coffee (or high-balls). In this novel, the truth is far more interesting. Sidney Brand may think he runs his studio, but women are working everywhere in Madge's Hollywood. The first place she lives in Hollywood is a women's "dorm" for Hollywood employees (a fictionalized Hollywood Studio Club). While many are "extra girls on the break for the big chance, frighteningly young for the most part and devastatingly pretty," she notes that there are also "an odd sprinkling of stenographers, script girls, assistant cutters, designers, a librarian or two and one honest-to-goodness writer who has actually had her name on screen credits but is very Scotch in makeup and is saving her money against a rainy day." The novel's penny-pinching writer is particularly apt, given that writers were struggling to secure union recognition and that it was well-known that the average Hollywood writer made less than a secretary during the 1930s (and this includes Shore and Lardner!).

So, does this mean *I Lost My Girlish Laughter* offers a rare feminist view of the film business way back in 1938? The opening pages reveal a surprisingly frank perspective. Although, as Madge admits in one letter to her girlfriend back in New York, "I still have something in me of the old guard feminists who broke out in bloomers and smashed windows," she keeps her subversiveness to herself and a few trusted girlfriends. Sidney Brand may claim he wants to know the "female angle," but, as readers soon discover, that respect and commitment to equality is unreliable at best, for *I Lost My Girlish Laughter* goes on to parody the studios' devotion to female audiences. Though Brand changes the name of his next big film project from *Sinners in Asylum* (an adaptation of a recent New York play by a writer who vehemently and repeatedly denies being a communist—to

great comic effect) to *Lady in a Cage*, Sarya Tarn's failure to win
over audiences at a disastrous preview precipitates yet another
change. The producer quickly renames it *That Gentleman from
the South* and recuts the footage to emphasize Tarn's unknown
male costar. The incident was loosely based on Schulman and
Lardner's terrible experiences with Marlene Dietrich during
the production of *The Garden of Allah* (1936). Demanding divas
often spelled financial catastrophe for film companies. As Lardner fumed at the time: "This whole picture has been a frightful
mess from the beginning . . . a lower, more underhanded woman
never existed than Marlene Dietrich. . . . She has a pernicious
influence on the morale of the whole organization."

But the novel's chaotic production history for *Sinners in
Asylum/ Lady in a Cage/ That Gentleman from the South* also gen-
erates wider questions about Selznick's intent in making a film
such as *Gone with the Wind*. Was it intended and marketed as
a women's picture because it focuses on protagonist Scarlett
O'Hara's experience—or because the gorgeous Mr. Gable plays
Rhett Butler? Schulman knew the score: the studio producers
understood that sexy male stars were even more important than
strong female content in attracting female filmgoers.

Madge is equally skeptical about women's own lack of solidarity in Hollywood's competitive marketplace. The film business
may have offered women the best chance of earning professional
respect and a decent wage in Depression-era America, but all
women certainly didn't treat one another equally. In *I Lost My
Girlish Laughter*, actresses, unless they are in supporting roles
or are bit players, are self-obsessed snobs and won't talk to
lowly secretaries like Madge. Sarya Tarn is hired for Brand's
next picture after they meet while he's at "a conference" in
Palm Springs. When Madge comes to work on her first day, she
finds that she has displaced another secretary (likely based on

workplace rival Marcella Bannett Rabwin) who allegedly slept
with Brand in hopes of a promotion. Women in Brand's organization are sometimes hired for their college educations but,
just as often, use the casting couch to get ahead. This certainly
isn't Madge's way, but it's a strategy that works for some. It's to
Madge's credit that, though she loses her "girlish laughter," she
doesn't become a total Hollywood cynic. In the end, she keeps
both her feminism and her sense of humor. She pities the other
secretary, banks rejected "Christmas" negligees intended for
Mrs. Brand (a swipe at the industry's efforts to mask its Jewish
heritage), admires the self-serving verve of a young supporting
actress, and watches the downfall of Ms. Tarn with equanimity.
If she has to stage a riot at a movie theater in order to prevent
film critics from seeing *Lady in a Cage* or fantasizes newspaper
headlines about attacking her boss when he won't give her a
lunch break or is asked about the "female angle" in script meetings by clueless male writers—well, it's all in a day's work. And
Madge's workdays are sometimes sixteen-plus hours.

Writing *I Lost My Girlish Laughter* was a risky venture.
Brand was so recognizably Selznick (right down to the producer's "Southern" film production and crisis over getting MGM
to loan Gable), and Selznick was MGM cofounder Louis B.
Mayer's son-in-law. Going after Selznick was tantamount to
going after MGM, Hollywood's richest, glitziest studio. But
there was no way of telling whether the book's popularity and
box office potential would mitigate its controversy. Other studio
heads might gleefully option the material to the detriment of
a rival, or they might close ranks and blackball it. If the press
got wind of Shore's involvement in the novel, her Hollywood
career would be truly over. The stakes were higher for Schulman. Although by the time the manuscript was finished, she
had quit her job with Selznick, become Silvia Lardner, and was

expecting her first child, she still had hopes of going back to work as a screenwriter. If she used her own name in publishing *I Lost My Girlish Laughter*, she would, as the saying goes, "never have lunch in that town again." Her husband's new career as a writer would also be at stake. Admittedly, there were other possibilities: the novel could be so popular that she would make more money than they could spend, reboot her career as a screenwriter like her husband, or simply take a leaf out of her famous father-in-law's book (Ring Lardner Sr.) and become the next great American humorist. Schulman duly concocted the pen name, Jane Allen, with Shore. But all her life, Schulman had been a fun-loving risk-taker. After all, once upon a time she came out to Hollywood just like Madge—without knowing a soul. On a certain level, she didn't care if the press discovered her identity.

When the book neared completion, they quietly contacted Margaret Mitchell's agent, Annie Laurie Williams, whom Schulman had met during Selznick's negotiations for *Gone with the Wind*. Williams recognized that she had the publishing sensation of 1938 in her hands and negotiated serialization with popular magazine *Cosmopolitan* before Random House printed the novel in the spring of 1938. When Schulman collected her $1,125 serialization check and the advance on the novel (about $20,000 in today's currency), Lardner acknowledged she "shows signs of becoming the leading breadwinner in our ménage." Her original idea paid off. New York critics raved that the book had "a laugh on every page" and that Madge's comments on the industry were "masterpieces in humor and irony." Margaret Mitchell loved the book so much that she read it twice. But, as she confided to friend Susan Myrick (technical advisor on Selznick's adaptation of *Gone with the Wind*), she "got a great deal more out of it" from her second reading. Myrick had sent

Mitchell a letter describing a chaotic *GWTW* script meeting involving Ben Hecht and John Van Druten. The situation "was identical with one in [*I Lost My Girlish Laughter*]" and sent her "into gales of laughter." The national press gleefully pointed out the satirical portrait of Selznick, drew unflattering comparisons between Sarya Tarn and the latest haughty foreign import to Hollywood, Hedy Lamarr, and made guesses about the identities of the other cast members. No other Hollywood novel had ever been quite so defiantly transparent about naming names. The buzz increased when journalists broke Schulman's cover and identified her as the author. Curiously, Jane Shore's name did not appear in these articles—perhaps because her authorial contribution was superficial compared to Schulman's, or perhaps because Shore still hoped to revive her Hollywood career once the film rights were secured and believed anonymity would eventually work in her favor.

The novel generated still more headlines when Orson Welles, already known for sensation-making stunts like the notorious October 1938 *War of the Worlds* broadcast, bought the radio rights. Much to Selznick's chagrin, Welles's Campbell Playhouse adaptation aired on CBS in January 1939—devilishly timed to coincide with principal photography on *Gone with the Wind*. In addition to Welles's own slick portrayal of the self-obsessed Brand, audiences were teased with a purported interview with the book's author, "Jane Allen." In his version, however, neither Madge nor her pseudonymous creators were the stars of the show. The radio adaptation replaced Madge as first-person narrator (played by Ilka Chase) with Brand. In Welles's view, male geniuses were more important than lowly secretaries.

Movie-minded columnists were divided over actresses Joan Blondell or Jean Arthur in the lead role (both had played versions of the plucky secretary on-screen in the 1930s), but, sadly, a film version never materialized, thanks in part to Selznick's pull with his father-in-law and, as Schulman put it in a letter to her mother-in-law Ellis Lardner, "a great reluctance on the part of producers here to buy a property blasting one of the boys." At one point early on, it had looked as though MGM would buy it—but very likely to prevent other studios from making it. Schulman went on to reveal that the story editor at MGM (very likely Lillie Messenger, formerly at RKO) "has threatened to wring my neck and . . . is swearing by all the stars that Metro will buy the book over her dead body." So much for female solidarity! When the Hollywood offers failed to materialize, Schulman and her husband pursued the idea of cowriting a Broadway adaptation. Producer Jed Harris had expressed interest. Private letters in the Lardner family indicate that Shore balked at developing the stage version and relations soured between the two writers. Any idea of a future partnership likely broke down when Schulman discovered Shore had only put her own name down as author in the novel's U.S. copyright filing following the book's publication in May 1938.

Shore would continue to use the "Jane Allen" pseudonym when she sold "A Girl's Best Friend Is Wall Street" to *Cosmopolitan* and secured the film deal with Columbia Pictures in 1940. But if the studio thought it was buying material from Schulman, they were wrong: *She Knew All the Answers* (1941) was no *I Lost My Girlish Laughter*. Nor was *Thanks God! I'll Take It From Here*, Shore's second Hollywood novel, cowritten by May Livingstone (Faber, 1946), which, as another film historian has noted, was surprisingly lifeless and pedestrian, despite some tacked-on memos toward the end of the story reminiscent of *I Lost My Girlish Laughter*'s format. But Shore at least scored another film deal: RKO transformed her novel about a novelist's foray into the motion picture business into *Without Reservations* (1946). The film was notable only for pairing Claudette Colbert and John Wayne.

Schulman's royalty checks dwindled, but her husband had writing stints at Warner Bros. and RKO. Things were tough for the couple at first; few were interested in buying the work of the husband of an infamous Hollywood turncoat like Silvia Schulman. For her part, Schulman tinkered with short stories and the dramatization of the novel with Lardner but concentrated on raising her two children, Peter and Ann. She was not nostalgic about her Hollywood career. As she remarked: "For years I put on a good show as a glorified hired hand." She preferred being in charge, even if the paychecks weren't as steady, and contemplated turning her skill with interior design into a paying career. Like her heroine Madge, she was petite, vivacious, and a survivor. "My mind's alive," she wrote to her mother-in-law, and, as she put it simply, "I've started growing up." The family finances improved after MGM bought Lardner's script with Michael Kanin, *Woman of the Year* (1942), but by then the Schulman-Lardner marriage had already fallen apart. They divorced in 1945, and Schulman kept the children and the family home.

Ironically, it was Irene and David Selznick who had initially urged her not to marry a non-Jewish man, stating that mixed marriages never worked. But the marriage didn't fail over religious reasons. Schulman was never a drinker and felt out of place and slightly skeptical among Lardner's hard-drinking, far-left writing cronies. She and her former spouse remained friends, and she occasionally sent Lardner suggestions for stories to develop. She would go back to work as an interior designer and building contractor, establishing a successful business. She was the only woman on the masthead of the California-based Hale

Company Builders during the 1950s and loved building houses as much as she had loved writing her novel. She married again in 1955 and divorced in 1960 but kept working, slyly remarking to her first husband, "I seem to have the talent for being a self-supporting ex-wife." With the exception of Sylvia Jarrico (wife of screenwriter Paul Jarrico) and Annie Laurie Williams, her Hollywood friends had melted away long ago, and as time passed, she rarely discussed the old days. But Schulman's house was always full of books, and it must have been a bittersweet day when her kids were old enough to take the copy of *I Lost My Girlish Laughter* down from the shelf and read it for themselves. Schulman lived to see Peter and Ann become academics and publish their own books. She died of cancer in 1993.

Looking back eighty years later, it's hard not to regret that *I Lost My Girlish Laughter* never made it to the big screen. The novel was published in an era when women still had some power in Hollywood and is a testimony to the myths and realities of the "female angle" of the motion picture business during Hollywood's golden age. It is a shame Harry Cohn of Columbia Pictures (famous for courting controversy and hiring women filmmakers) didn't option it for his star Jean Arthur; she would have been superb as Madge. And if he hired Schulman to write the script with his onetime contract writer Mary C. McCall Jr.—and Dorothy Arzner (herself once a lowly Hollywood secretary) to direct; Columbia editor Viola Lawrence to cut; and Cohn's favorite executive, Virginia Van Upp, in charge of production—what could have been better? *I Lost My Girlish Laughter* is one of Hollywood's tragic lost opportunities.

Although the novel was reprinted in the 1950s in cheap paperback editions, with cover art exaggerating the lurid sexual escapades of the motion picture people, few literary critics took notice of what was inside the covers. "Jane Allen" and *I Lost My*

Girlish Laughter vanished from cultural consciousness. Instead, Hollywood novels written by men—Nathanael West, F. Scott Fitzgerald (*The Last Tycoon*, 1941), and Budd Schulberg (*What Makes Sammy Run?*, 1941)—became the canonical standards of the great Hollywood novel of this period. Madge Lawrence was completely upstaged by Fitzgerald's doomed mogul Monroe Stahr (based on MGM's boy-genius, Irving Thalberg) and Schulberg's double-crossing screenwriter Sammy Glick. These novels had cultural afterlives as films (*The Day of the Locust*, dir. John Schlesinger, 1975; *The Last Tycoon*, dir. Elia Kazan, 1976), musicals (*What Makes Sammy Run?*, 1964–65, 2006), and television series (*What Makes Sammy Run?*, Philco Television Playhouse, 1949, NBC Sunday Showcase, 1959; *The Last Tycoon*, Amazon Prime Video, 2016–17). Ironically, Selznick's *A Star Is Born* has now been through four big-budget film versions (1937, 1954, 1976, and 2018), a testimony in part to the enduringly popular view of Svengali-esque men molding a pretty face into a star.

Perhaps now, with renewed interest in women in Hollywood, it's time to take notice of Madge Lawrence and what she had to say about the women who ran Hollywood behind the scenes so many years ago.

—*J. E. Smyth*

Principal Characters

MADGE LAWRENCE
Her ambition was to get into movies—
she did—but not the way you think!

SIDNEY BRAND
High-pressure producer to whom
figures mean nothing—except those of girls.

MYRTLE STANDISH
A blonde, china-blue eyes, lovely;
still a bit-player until—

JIM PALMER
Works in publicity, *plays* at
being a Hollywood "wolf."

SARYA TARN
Beautiful Viennese actress who is in
danger of sleeping her way *out* of stardom.

BRUCE ANDERS
"Gorgeous" male who goes to Hollywood to star—
but he "goes Hollywood," too!

I LOST MY
GIRLISH
LAUGHTER

1

I Become a Proletarian

HOLLYWOOD, CALIFORNIA   OCTOBER 10

MISS AGNES LAWRENCE

KANSAS CITY MO

ARRIVED SAFELY STOP STAYING AT GIRLS CLUB STOP
KNOW YOU WILL BE DELIGHTED HEAR WE ARE PUT TO
BED AT TEN OCLOCK STOP LOVE

MADGE

GIRLS' COMMUNITY CLUB
HOLLYWOOD, CALIFORNIA

October 10

Mr. Marc Freeman,
National Studios,
Hollywood, California.

Dear Mr. Freeman:

I am enclosing a letter of introduction which was given to me by Robert James.

May I hope for an interview?

Very truly yours,
Madge Lawrence

October 20

Liz, my pet:

Your letter, dog-eared and worn, limped in from Kansas City and contacted me here. It served as a sweetly steadying anchor to the wind after ten white-hot days of dizzying sunshine and abruptly chilled nights. I'm beginning to understand why the hot, hot tropics can do a white woman in. That interesting New York pallor of mine is a cute rosy red except in places where a large fat brown freckle is parked. My hair has degenerated into a stringy frenzy which no amount of brushing will curb. My svelte, not-an-ounce-overweight-size-twelve chassis has developed suddenly bumptious symptoms that are definitely alarming and altogether I don't seem to coordinate physically. There is nothing about me, in fact, that is familiar and reassuring any longer and over all, that glaring, searing white sun. God, how I yearn for a clean rain-swept afternoon around Washington Square!

The club where I am stopping temporarily is merely a sop to Aunt Agnes's concern over her orphan niece. She knew someone who knew someone who met someone else who told her that all the nice girls stay here in this friendly, homey atmosphere which is cheap, safe and secure. At that, it's not a bad little hostelry although it simply crawls with femmes and wherever a mob of femmes gather there is something depressing about the atmosphere. I wouldn't for the world admit that to a gentleman, because I still have something in me of the old guard feminists who broke out in bloomers and smashed windows.

This little refuge which was built on the largesse of movie money to make Hollywood safe for stray girls is ever so Spanish, with white stucco walls and patios and cells glaringly clean and equally cheerless. There are ninety of us here, all career-bound in pictures but in the tadpole stage. The majority are extra girls on the break for the big chance, frighteningly young for the most part and devastatingly pretty. There is an odd sprinkling of stenographers, script girls, assistant cutters, designers, a librarian or two and one honest-to-goodness writer who has actually had her name on screen credits but is very Scotch in makeup and is saving her money against a rainy day. I'd like to know her better but she walks in a little aura of her own, so very aloof and grand, for I've discovered that socially, as the picture colony evaluation goes, she is worlds away from us. I'm panting to ask her how it feels up there but she no speaka the English to us.

I have sent out my letters of introduction but apparently no one has taken time out to recognize that fact.

My love to Momma and Poppa Rocco and all the little Roccos of Rocco's Grotto. How is Tony doing on the violin?

Ever,
Maggie

October 21

Dear Aunt Agnes:

Thanks for your wire, but your worries are needless. I'm very fat and sassy. Would have written you sooner but rather hoped to have good news for you and didn't want to write until I did.

Nothing so far has turned up. I had several letters of introduction from people back in New York and sent them all off to studios but I haven't had so much as a nibble. The studio people must be so busy.

The club is charming and they take ever so good care of us. It's perfectly scrumptious to look at, Spanish in architecture with darling patios and beautiful flowers, though they don't smell very much.

The girls here are very chummy and helpful. They just adore that green sports outfit you gave me and several of them have worn it for important engagements. It was too snug for one of them but she didn't mind at all. She just let out the seams and dropped the hem. It is too bad I haven't an assortment of evening clothes for there is a definite need of them here. It seems a lot of business engagements take place in the evening. However, I'm doing my humble best with what I have to donate to the cause.

They're awfully jolly about letting you run a bill here, so I don't have to worry for a while yet.

Enjoyed so much my short visit with you. Write soon.

Your loving niece,

Madge

October 22

Miss Madge Lawrence,
Girls' Community Club,
Hollywood, California.

Dear Miss Lawrence:

Mr. Freeman has asked me to acknowledge your letter and to advise you he regrets there is no opening at the present in which he could place you. I would suggest you apply to our Employment Department. I am sure they will show you every courtesy.

Yours very truly,
Ellen Flagg
SECRETARY TO MARC FREEMAN

October 22

Mr. Robert James,
Daily News,
New York City.

Dear Bob:

The enclosed is the reply I received from your friend, Marc Freeman, when I sent him your letter of introduction.

You were a darling to give me the letter and I really appreciated it. His response was positively encouraging compared to most who didn't bother to answer at all. So much for all letters of introduction.

I took Miss Flagg's advice and tried to make an appointment with the Employment Department. They wrote saying Miss Flagg had sent them my name and that it had been entered on their lists and when and if ever there was an opening, they would let me know.

I've decided that Employment Departments are no way to get into studios.

How are all the boys in the back room doing?

Maggie

Sunday, October 29

Liz:

You might as well climb into your best nightie, open a new package of cigarets, get a long highball, and cast yourself on something soft because this is going to be a long scenario—and don't peek at the last page because it has a surprising denouement.

Place: Hollywood. *Time:* It is eight o'clock last Friday evening and I am sitting in my room in this manless Eden gnawing my nails and trying to decide between a good book and a cheap movie. Around me the chirp of crickets and the high girlish laughter of nearly ninety voices (the rest are out on dates) and the jeering of phones. Did you ever notice how a phone positively jeers when you don't know anybody and you're not likely to be on the receiving end of the line? Odd about phones in a place like this. They're the punctuation marks in an otherwise meaningless existence; the live contact-points with a living world outside these veritable convent walls. Anyhow, I am sitting here and thinking I will go stark, staring mad and musing in my maudlinity on how I would give anything to be at Joe Rocco's Grotto on MacDougal Street with you and the others and wondering whatever possessed me to think I had a call to Hollywood, when suddenly the soul within me revolts. So, setting my old black felt at a jaunty angle, I saunter forth alone into the night.

I travel along Vine Street by foot until I come to Mr. Levy's Tavern. I have read about Mr. Levy's Tavern in the papers sev-

I LOST MY GIRLISH LAUGHTER

eral times and pause there. That proves my downfall. For the sound of merriment within and the clinking of glasses produce a nostalgia I cannot ignore. Accordingly, I push through those swinging doors. The bar is crowded, so I modestly hie me to a little table facing the bar. I have taken the third sip of my Scotch highball and am feeling very sorry for myself when suddenly I spy a familiar face and hear a familiar voice. My first reaction is a wild surge of joy at recognizing anyone I know; then I think why couldn't it have been someone I liked. For, it is no other than that limp bore, Bob Faulkner. Don't tell me! I know what you're thinking. But, in my condition even Bob Faulkner is welcome. Do you remember how we used to devise every known dodge at State to avoid him? Well, I think my sins are coming home to roost, for now I feel a large grin of welcome sprouting on my face and I wave frantically. He doesn't seem to see me so I wave the louder. I am sure he looks directly at me but it is as though his eyes are opaque and they see nothing. I am thinking it is all very odd when I notice that a man near him is nudging him and pointing to me and whispering. Suddenly Bob comes to life. Next thing I know he is beside me and introducing me to Max Sellers, the director. Mr. Sellers is very cordial to me and Bob is very much Bob. The moment I am with him I am thinking why did I bother. Loneliness isn't worth that sacrifice. But Mr. Sellers is already paying me some dubious compliments and I am suddenly aware of the fact that I am wearing an old hat and that I didn't powder my nose and it is hours since I applied any lipstick and besides I have runs in my hose. Mr. Sellers is saying it is so refreshing to meet a girl like me in Hollywood and what am I doing here and by now I am having another drink and telling him all!

Mr. Sellers is most sympathetic. He says isn't it a coincidence but just today he heard of a very fine job as secretary to Sidney

Brand, the producer, and I will fit the bill because Mr. Brand believes in the higher education and won't have anything less than a college girl as his secretary. That leaves me somewhat limp because it is the first time anyone has been interested in my higher education. The job, says Mr. Sellers, is practically mine for he and Mr. Brand are just like! He crosses one finger over another. I just burst with gratitude and then Mr. Sellers says we must all celebrate my new job. I remonstrate Mr. Brand doesn't know me but Mr. Sellers says it is in the bag. Just to prove it he will telephone Mr. Brand in Palm Springs. It is all cockeyed and a funny way to get hired but before we are three more drinks along, we have had Palm Springs on the wire and I am *in*!

We must go on to the Cocoanut Grove, says Mr. Sellers and I must call him Max and he will introduce me to Hollywood. It will be in the nature of a debut. I demur. I murmur something about how I am not properly dressed for such an occasion, leaving people to suppose if I could just dash home I could change into something definitely chic for the event. I do not tell the truth, my love, which is that I haven't anything chic in my wardrobe with the exception of my green outfit and that is out on loan for the next three nights. Fortunately, it seems Mr. Sellers is above such things. He would be proud, says he, to take me anywhere in town just as I am. I begin to think Mr. Sellers is a man above all men.

I will have to confess that by the time Mr. Sellers's (Max's) white Packard touring car has deposited us at the Ambassador Hotel, I am in something of a fog. There is a very gay long awning all decked out in colored lights and I feel a little bit like Alice in Wonderland. I suddenly am aware that Bob is no longer in our company. I comment on this and Mr. Sellers makes a grimace. Bob is a good man on the set, he says, and one of the best assistants he ever had. But he is a heel. Did I notice that he didn't seem to recognize me at first? I did. Well, says Mr. Sellers, that was kleig myopiaritis. And what is that, I ask, very puzzled. Patiently, Mr. Sellers explains that people who are "in" in Hollywood don't like to recognize old friends for fear that they might want something. That is a new idea and gives me pause for thought.

But I do not ponder for long. I don't get a chance. For there are mobs of people pouring through the lobby toward the Cocoanut Grove, wearing the dizziest kind of clothes and I cannot help recognizing a flock of celebrities. Is it always like this? I ask. This is Star Night at the Grove, I am informed. Somebody then waves to Mr. Sellers and I see it is a well-known screen actress and she is wearing a gown of white slipper satin with a litter of fox furs slung over her shoulders in the form of a cape. It is most effective. Her long yellow hair is as smooth and shiny as her gown. I get a definitely hollow feeling. I know it is the female in me and I feel very shabby and down-at-heel. Please, I say to Mr. Sellers, if we must go in could we have a table where no one can see us. Anything I want, says Mr. Sellers. But the lass of the yellow hair has hooked her arm into Mr. Sellers and she is crooning in a lovely husky voice, "Hello, Max darling. Why don't you join us? Gary is here with me." It isn't until then that I notice a very beautiful young man whose face is not familiar to me. I am introduced. The blonde lovely, whose name I cannot mention for reasons you will understand later, is very polite to me but frankly puzzled. I begin to think maybe my petticoat is showing. Then Gary is saying "Howdeyoud" in a very Christ College accent and I suddenly remember reading somewhere about a new English star who is making his debut opposite the blonde.

The answer to all that is we get a ringside table willy-nilly.

It is some moments before I get my bearings and even then I think I am in a nightmare . . . you know like the dream where the rector comes to call and all you have on is a nightgown. The Grove is an enormous place and hundreds of people are jammed in. There are trees all around! Palm trees with cocoanuts and stuffed monkeys. I think I am seeing things so I decide to have another drink.

We are all very gay and Mr. Sellers seems to think I am something of a wit. He is very devoted. Even Gary unbends and pays me some attention. I expand and my female soul is very happy indeed.

A lot of people who are dancing by stop at the table to say hello, but to Mr. Sellers's annoyance they do not seem to notice me. Because, he hisses behind his hand, I am no celebrity or at least a beautiful chorus girl, people think I am a nobody. Well, he will show me what makes the wheels go round in this village and how phony it all is. We will fool everyone. So when a very prominent producer stops by with his wife, who is a star, they say hello to Mr. Sellers, the blonde and Gary. Then Mr. Sellers says "And, of course, you know Madge Lawrence?" They hesitate for a split second and then shake my hand vigorously. "Of course," they say. So we continue this little game and will you believe it? Without exception all these important film people say, "Of course . . . yes . . . how do you do. . . ." Mr. Sellers chuckles. You are a celebrity now, he whispers to me.

I am still thinking, though, that I don't relish all this publicity when the music stops and they shoot a spotlight on our table. A thousand eyes turn to us and I want to crawl under the table. I must be a sight by this time. The blonde gets up and gets off a beautiful little speech. It seems she is the star of the night. The English actor is then introduced and everybody applauds. Mr. Sellers then takes a bow. Then all around me I hear little whispers. "But who is she? But who is she?" They mean me, I discover!

I figure it is a shame to torture them like this so I put my finger to my lips and whisper to the people at the next table, "Pst! I am Sally Rand—in mufti!"

My public is amused. Mr. Sellers is amused. He explains it to Gary, who is also amused. But the blonde doesn't move a muscle. In fact, the blonde doesn't seem to like me very much. She would like to leave she tells Gary haughtily. He is quite happy here, he says, which leads to a little argument. But the Britisher sets his jaw and is stubborn. I am very admiring because it is my first face-to-face encounter with the English and I think to myself it is spirit like this which built the Empire! Then the blonde lets loose a string of very low but effective epithets. I am appalled. I am outraged. You know how dignified I am in my cups. I am not, I say haughtily to Mr. Sellers, in the habit of associating with fishwives. Will he please ask the lady to leave. Mr. Sellers doesn't understand about this dignity of mine so he thinks I am terrific and guffaws loudly. The blonde is now really aroused. We are at an impasse! So Mr. Sellers whispers to Gary to take the lady home and join us later if he likes. As the blonde leaves with Gary everyone breaks out in applause. I think it is most ironic.

Mr. Sellers and I do not stay much longer, as he thinks I ought to make a really proper debut and go on to the Trocadero. In no time at all, the white Packard deposits us there. We go down into the Trocadero "cellar" which is very chummy though large. I like it much better because with its pine walls and red leather seats, it is less fancy than the Grove, and besides the people look more like human beings.

There are a number of gentlemen stagging it around the bar, which I think is selfish of them, for Hollywood is swarming with ladies who are very agreeable and they ought to do something about it. Mr. Sellers must be popular because they come over to our table and pay me some very elaborate compliments. Mr. Sellers whispers to me that he has a bad reputation and these gentlemen think I am the new favorite and are therefore paying court to me. They all want something, he says a little despondently.

A dark vivacious young lady, in the most elegant sports outfit I have ever seen, comes tripping over to the table with four very effeminate escorts and when she is introduced to me I recognize her. She is a celebrated Follies beauty whose tour de force is a devastating frankness backed up by a million dollar divorce settlement. We all have a very gay time indeed and I am feeling that I am "in" when the dark lady cracks out with "And what do you do in pictures, Miss Lawrence?"

"I am a secretary," I say happily.

She stares at me as though I am a bad joke. I am like Alice when she steps back through the looking glass, and I feel myself shrinking to my normal size.

"What a terrible way to make a living," she says coldly. I am sober. I realize then that this is a dream and that I am after all only a member of the proletariat.

Love,
Maggie

P.S. Mr. Sellers is also a married man. Isn't that sad?

2

What a Terrible Way to Make a Living

FROM A SECRETARY'S PRIVATE JOURNAL

October 30

Up and at 'em this morning bright and early. Am very excited at the prospect of starting off in this lucrative motion-picture business; also most curious about the place and people with whom I have to work. By dint of cajolery and threat snag back my best green outfit and bedeck myself as I think fitting for a girl on the verge of a new life.

By bribing a lass with a delicate air (she was hung-over) with a loan of my silver evening sandals, I get a lift in a Model T Ford out to the studio. My chauffeurette who is on saluting terms with the grizzled guardian of the gates waves me into a reception office and buzzes off to the casting department.

Here I spend several frantic minutes impressing upon a thoroughly disagreeable page boy that I am Sidney Brand's new secretary and rate a little time. He, neither impressed nor very quick to please, runs an appraising eye or two over me.

"I hope I am the type," I snap out shrewishly.

"Oh, you'll do," he drawls back, then deigns to escort me across the courtyard to my working quarters.

Am almost blinded by the blazing white sunshine striking against the everlasting white walls and hurtling back with a stunning fury. Against this, blobs of too-red flowers and the parched green of palm trees barely moving in a mild breeze.

Past stages and bungalows. In the shade lounge dancing girls in briefs; men in dress suits with bibs under their chins to protect their white shirts and collars from greasepaint; peasants, soldiers, idlers all taking a brief respite from hot sound stages. Up the end of the walk is a parking rectangle filled with Fiats, Duesenbergs, Cadillacs, and Fords from which pour a stream of people spreading in all directions. Laborers career by on noisy little handcars narrowly missing pedestrians; electricians drag huge lights and cables; men move scenery. On the side stretches a row of barracks housing bit players; apart from them modern white bungalows where roost studio royalty—the stars.

We are enveloped suddenly in a whirring hum, the inane disjointed rise of voices, the blare of music, emanating from a group of buildings to the left. I stop for a moment to listen. The page boy grins. "I'll show you something," he says and pulls me into a half-open door, at the same time insuring my silence by placing a finger to his lips.

Up a few stairs and we enter a small dim booth filled with a mass of intricate machinery humped in the darkness like so many diabolic shapes. I have a weird nightmarish sensation until I make out the figure of a very mild-looking young man who tends these eerie devices—the projectionist.

An opening between two machines permits us to stand and peer in through a tiny window down into a small theater. The screen is blank but from it emanate ghostly voices and music. I am a bit startled. The page seems to enjoy my discomfiture.

Out once more in the sunlight I breathe freely. The page

chuckles. That's how the sound in a film is checked, he explains. It's run off on a separate roll. It's only the public who wants the actors, he adds contemptuously.

On until we halt in front of a cheery New England cottage growing all over with vines and flowers and fronted by a well-tended lawn. It might be Massachusetts but for the small incongruity of a few palm trees. This I think must be a film set, only to learn it is the headquarters for the Sidney Brand Production Unit. The page boy and I part company here.

All is still as a tomb in the bungalow; not a sign of life about. Boldly I make my way through half a dozen offices and though I find the windows complete with Venetian blinds and attractive chintz drapes I am a little disappointed not to find even one spinning wheel. I had heard these people were more thorough.

My lone tour of inspection ends back in the reception room where I find a very pert young brunette with her hat on the back of her head, sitting behind the desk and with the aid of a pocket mirror propped up in front of her anxiously examining her nose for blackheads.

She is very startled to see me, as though surprised to find anything else vaguely human prowling about these parts. Learn later that but few of the staff show up before ten or eleven as there is a great deal of night work here.

"I am Madge Lawrence," I say brightly, "and I was hired last night as Mr. Brand's secretary."

"Now that is a new dodge," she says, not removing her eyes from the mirror. "Mr. Brand is in Palm Springs and has been there the last few days."

"There are telephones," I offer loftily. "Mr. Sellers used one last night."

"Max Sellers!"

I nod.

She now condescends to give me her full attention.

"Well," she allows doubtfully after a pause, "you don't look like that sort."

"That," I say, nettled, "is strictly a private matter between my Maker and me. Incidentally and notwithstanding I work for a living."

"Okay!" She grinningly capitulates and gives me a beautifully manicured hand to shake. "My name is Amanda Flowers."

I think it is a joke but she delivers it straight.

Her job she says is to keep agents, actors and other such rodents out of our hair. That is, she protects me and I in turn do my darndest best to protect Mr. Brand so that he can carry on his creative work without undue disturbances.

I am being initiated into the office routine and examining the files when there is a noisy interruption. It is a callow youth wearing a loud plaid sports coat, contrasting trousers and a gaucho shirt. I am trying to decide which one of the rodents he is and figure him at least for a greasepaint addict when I am introduced to him as our office boy.

He emits a startled whistle. "Hello! Gee, will Maxine be sore. She thought she had this job cinched."

"Pipe down, big shot. Show Miss Lawrence her office."

I am led into my own office, a small but pleasant room, boasting some comfortable chairs, a few really good etchings and a handsome desk bearing up under two telephones, a dictograph, and a secretary's dictaphone receiving set.

Bud proves obliging and anxious to make good with me, albeit he passes off a few "nifties" and pauses for laughs while regaling me with the lowdown on the "right people" in the studio and a smattering of dirt about some of the glamour boys and girls.

We are examining Mr. Brand's office when he tells me he can put me on to a good thing. If I place some money right on the nose of Ladybird in the third race at Tanforan, I can earn a couple of permanents. I thank him kindly but put him off, saying I have too much on my mind today to think about horse racing.

"Okay. But any time you feel the pinch let me know and I'll pass on something good, and I mean good. The boss himself comes to me for tips."

I must look my incredulity for he laughs indulgently.

"Ask Amanda. You see . . ." he leans forward confidentially and pauses to take my measure in full as though trying to make up his mind whether I am worthy of his confidence. Apparently I pass muster for he goes on with a rush. "It's part of my system. I'm not going to be an office boy always. I'm gonna be somebody in Hollywood one of these days. So what do I do? I find out that the big shots are all gamblers—that's their weak spot. They'll gamble on anything but particularly on horses. So I make it my business to know about horses."

He pauses portentously. I still do not understand what horses have to do with becoming an executive in Hollywood and must show my ignorance for he shakes his head sadly.

"Y'see contacts is the important thing in this town. I get the dope on horses and I'm good. I make money. So I let everybody know about it and pretty soon the executives come to me for tips. I'm pretty cagey about when and how I dish them out and pretty soon they see I'm good. So what? Everybody knows me. Now, when the psychological time comes and there is a good promotion, somebody is bound to think of me!"

I can see little logic in all this, but then I am new to the game, so who am I to dampen the ardor of an ambitious young man? But I am relieved of the necessity of making any comment for Bud yells at somebody outside the window and is off.

Return to my own office and private reveries only to be rudely interrupted by the ominous ring of the phone. It is Palm Springs and my boss on the wire.

"Find Palmer!" he yells excitedly, "and have him call me immediately."

Somehow I realize there is no point in mentioning the fact that I don't know Palmer and merely say, "Yes."

"Get your notebook," is his next command.

"I am ready," I say.

"Right . . . let's go . . ."

Thirty minutes and fifteen pages later, limp and exhausted, I hang up the phone and stare in bewilderment at the last page of pothooks—his final instructions.

FROM A STENOGRAPHER'S NOTEBOOK

Mr. B. arriving Thursday 3 P.M. have car meet him at station. Arrange appointment with chiropodist at studio—4 P.M.

Get Warner Bros. print of *Let's Make Hay* for screening S. B.'s home Thursday evening. *Maiden All Forlorn* unit available for screening. Me too.

Have Research Department check on hairdressers for Dietrich in *Maiden All Forlorn*. Also have them check on gags to be used in Russian barber shop before the Revolution.

Call Mrs. B. and advise S. B. returning.

Call Dietrich and arrange appointment with S. B.

Call Bullock's-Wilshire and have them send out samples of bedroom slippers—size 12C—no patent leather.

Send all issues of *Hollywood Reporter* and *Variety* home to Mrs. B.

Advise cutter to be ready for preview day or so.

Remind S. B. to call Joe Burns Friday morning.

Have S. B.'s tennis rackets checked for re-stringing . . . ready for weekend.

And don't forget to have Palmer call me!

I get my breath and holler for Amanda. Mutely I point to notebook. She is very consoling and advises me to relax. No one, she philosophizes, expects wonders—although she admits S. B. likes things done his way and his way is to do them immediately and against all odds. I wouldn't know how to perform even one of these little wonders, I say dispirited. Who is Palmer? Who is the cutter and where do I find him? What is *Maiden All Forlorn* and where do I find any Russian barber-shop gags before the Revolution?

Palmer is head of publicity. Holding Amanda's other explanations in check, phone Publicity Department. Palmer isn't there. Leave message—important for him to telephone S. B. in Palm Springs.

Maiden All Forlorn I learn is our new picture with Marlene Dietrich. *Let's Make Hay* is an old Warner Bros. picture with the same background and perhaps there is something worth watching in it, as it made a lot of money. The Research Department can worry along about Russian barber-shop gags. The cutter is the man who does just that, cuts films and pastes them together for the screen. It is more important than it sounds. A cutter can either make or ruin a picture and he rates a lot of money when he is good.

"But who," I ask, "can Joe Burns be?"

"Joe Burns," says Amanda, "is a scalp specialist, a wizard at restoring hair where there isn't any."

"Mr. Brand is bald then?" I ask solicitously.

"He has a lot on his mind," Amanda says cryptically.

Busy attending to these various chores and typing out letters during which time I have many interruptions. They are people who have come in to meet and welcome me. Think it is very sociable of them and am pleased and agreeable. Suddenly struck with thought that my callers are suspiciously predominantly male. This prompts questions on my part which elicit information that Bud has spread the news I am easy on the eyes and an "all right guy." That sets Buddy with me for I am not above a little flattery.

Realize it is twelve o'clock and no Palmer. Phone Publicity. Girl there advises I telephone dressing room of male star with whom he had appointment. Telephone and valet informs me Palmer never showed up. Try barber shop—Amanda's suggestion—no Palmer.

Look up from phone to see girl staring at me.

"Hello," I say blankly.

"I'm Maxine Stoddard," she says sweetly, and comes toward me.

"How do you do?" I say mechanically; then fogged brain clicks. This is young woman who expected my job. She is pretty with soft, naturally curly blonde hair. The female in me rears. It always does with that type but mentally slap myself for such reactionaryism.

"Well!" she says. "You are not the type I expected Mr. Brand to choose for a secretary. I am surprised!"

"I hope you are pleasantly surprised," I say coldly. "I am fed up on people discussing my type."

Fortunately Bud comes in and I am spared any more barbs.

"Hello, Maxine," he calls cheerfully. "Not bad for a brunette, is she?"

I think I detect a little malice there.

"You're an obnoxious brat," Maxine coos at him pleasantly. She starts to leave. "Let's have lunch together sometime," she calls from the door.

"You gotta watch her," Buddy advises when the door is closed. "She's hell on wheels and hates your guts already for tagging her job."

"Look here, Bud. I feel pretty rotten about this. It looks as though someone has let Maxine down badly."

"Don't waste your sympathy on her. She doesn't rate it."

I am curious to know more and making up my mind whether to question Bud or make it clear here and now that it is beneath my dignity to indulge in personalities, when the telephone rings.

It is Mr. Brand.

"Christ! Where is Palmer?"

"I have been trying to locate Mr. Palmer everywhere," I say, "but he isn't to be found."

"Don't tell me that. Get Palmer. Check with everyone on the lot but get him. Call out the fire department if necessary."

"Very well," I say meekly.

"Have any newspapermen called?" he goes on, his voice positively furtive.

"Why no, Mr. Brand."

"Thank God for that. If any of those interfering bastards call, you don't know anything—deny everything."

"Yes, Mr. Brand."

I hang up. Bud is standing there, his eyes glistening with excitement.

"Newspapermen, huh. Newspapermen—I'll bet it's something hot."

"How did you hear—?" I start.

"You could have heard him a mile away. Boy, I'll bet it's good. I'm gonna do a little investigating. . . ."

"You'll mind your own business," I say sharply, "and find Palmer."

I telephone Publicity—Publicity is busy. Drat Palmer. Why the devil doesn't he show up? Here I am faced with a crisis the first day of my career and this Palmer person has to cross me. If I don't find him maybe I'll be fired, I think darkly. I look at my watch. It is two o'clock. I remember I am hungry but I don't dare leave until I find Palmer.

Publicity calls me. Palmer hasn't been at the studio as far as they know. However I might try the commissary and then the gymnasium. If he isn't there . . . I now receive a list of telephone numbers. "Girl friends," giggles Publicity.

I call the commissary. It takes ten minutes to find out Palmer isn't there. My nerves begin to jingle; my stomach cries for sustenance. I call gymnasium. No Palmer.

I start calling the list of phone numbers.

"He was here this morning," simpers the second number on the list. "But he came and left on the run. He was very tight."

I go through the list. Some don't answer and the rest haven't seen Palmer. They are all females. "Philanderer," I hiss silently. I know I will loathe this man.

Bud comes in on the run.

"Boy, oh, boy, oh, boy!" he howls. "Is it good . . . is it terrific!"

"Stop it!" I yell. "I'm going mad without having to listen to that!"

"Yeah? Well get a load of this. S. B. is in plenty of a jam. He lams to Palm Springs for a conference—maybe. Anyhow this foreign dame is there—this actress Sarya Tarn. By accident— maybe. So he and Sarya go places and do things. Everything is dandy until late last night when they are in the gambling Casino, Brand gets into an argument with a guy over Sarya.

S. B. takes a sock at him. Camera! Flashlights! Newspapers! Get it?"

I am listening intently, but so far I don't see anything wrong with the scenario.

"I think Mr. Brand did the right thing," I say indignantly.

"Yeah? But you see there's Mrs. Brand and it don't look right for Mr. Brand to be away on business and get into fights over dames—especially foreign actresses. It will certainly look lousy in the papers."

"What can Mr. Palmer do?" I ask.

Bud is disgusted with me.

"Jim Palmer is an ex-newspaperman and knows everyone in the business. That is why he was hired. He can fix it so the papers tone down their story and Mr. Brand will look like a hero in an innocent fracas."

"How did you find all this out?" I ask suspiciously.

"I got sources," Bud throws out his chest and struts. "I'm not talking."

Well, there I am. Mr. Brand is in a jam. No Palmer. Bad publicity. No job for Maggie. I am desperate.

Amanda comes flying in. "I heard Palmer just arrived and is heading for the commissary. Maybe you can have a sandwich and Palmer, too."

I do not wait to hear any more. I grab Bud and fly, for I do not know where the commissary is.

Pell-mell we dash across the lot. Even before we get there, I can hear the clatter of dishes, the clang of silverware and an unholy babel of voices. We burst in. I have one flash of a mass of people, most of them in yellow makeup and costumes, and then a roar of laughter shatters my ears.

We push our way through the crowd that is jammed in and

around tables. The center of the room is cleared for action. Hopping around the arena on all fours is a man wearing horse's trappings. Astride his back is a jockey waving his cap and crying, "Yip . . . ee . . . Yip . . . ee . . ." What is it about? I whisper to Buddy. "Paying off a bet," he says.

Around and around they go several times. The crowd shouts. "Yip . . . ee . . . Yip . . . ee . . ." in chorus. Then the horse throws the jockey, picks up his hand, and cries, "Ladies . . . and gentlemen, the Winnah!" James Palmer!

I have found my man.

3

I Meet the Boss

GIRLS' COMMUNITY CLUB
HOLLYWOOD, CALIFORNIA

October 31

Dear Miss Lawrence:

I do not like to censure my girls about such things but I know you need only be reminded of your departure from the way we do things here not to permit a recurrence of last night.

Mary Emmett

Dear Mrs. Emmett:

I feel terribly guilty about last night and perhaps I may be vindicated in the fact that we were all celebrating my new job.

Regretfully,

Madge Lawrence

SUPER FILMS
INTER-OFFICE COMMUNICATION

To: *Madge Lawrence*   Subject: *Apology*
From: *James Palmer*   Date: *October 31*

Dear Miss Lawrence:

As you have doubtless seen by the papers, we saved the day for the dear old Alma Mater and Mr. Brand is enshrined in the hearts of womanhood the world over as a gallant, chivalrous knight of old who gave his all to preserve the good name of a lady.

However, I have an uneasy feeling that I gave you some very bad moments and considering it was your first day at the studio I can hardly expect your forgiveness. What rankles mainly is that you saw me thrown in the arena. It wounds my masculine ego and isn't exactly a fitting start to what I hope may become a pleasant association.

May I assure you of my good will and if there is anything I can do for you, just say the word.

James (Jockey) Palmer

SUPER FILMS
INTER-OFFICE COMMUNICATION

To: *James Palmer*   Subject: *My Problem*
From: *Madge Lawrence*   Date: *October 31*

Dear Mr. Palmer:

This is my first experience at working in a studio and I have come to the conclusion that I must take many odd things in my stride. My life hitherto, I realize, has been limited to very small horizons and sheltered lees. And talking of shelters, I have a boon to crave. So how about turning knight-errant for me? Amanda tells me that you're the boy wonder at accomplishing miracles and I'm urgently in need of one at the moment. (I mean the miracle.)

I want a place to live near the studio which will be pleasant, private, cheap and cheery. I've been putting up temporarily at the Girls' Community Club but am afraid my girlish efferves-cence is a jarring note. Last night I staged a little mild revelry for some of the inmates and myself to celebrate my new job. (You see I have my lapses too.) This morning I received a polite reprimand from Mrs. Emmett, the directress. I'm not in the habit of staging orgies as a regular thing but I do feel that when a girl has call to a little relaxation she should be privileged to do so. If you can make any suggestions I will be . . .

Most gratefully,
Madge Lawrence

November 1

Dear Aunt Agnes:

Wonderful news! I've got a job.

I'm secretary to Sidney Brand, the man whose pictures you don't like. It seems I was around the corner when opportunity showed up with Bob Faulkner, whom Elizabeth and I knew very well indeed at State University. Bob is now an assistant to Max Sellers, the important director, and when he heard I was looking for a job, introduced me to his chief who in turn arranged this position with Mr. Brand. Mr. Sellers said I had come to the right place for Hollywood, and Mr. Brand in particular is very appreciative of college educations.

Oddly enough—but then this is a town of oddities—I haven't

even met Mr. Brand. It seems he is away at Palm Springs with his writers working on a new screenplay. This is a very hard-working community and important people like Mr. Brand often have to travel hundreds of miles where they can work in peace.

It may interest you to know that I saw Colin Grove lunching at the studio yesterday and he is even more handsome off the screen than on. If you will be a nice auntie and write me often, I might even get him to autograph a picture for you and just think—how all your friends in the bridge club will envy you.

I have enjoyed so much being at the Club but because the studio is so far away and transportation facilities unreliable, I am forced to find a place to live near the studio. One of our publicity men is even now on the lookout for an apartment for me. In the meantime address your letters to me at the studio.

Love,

Madge

Val Mar Apartments

November 4

Dear Liz:

Sometimes I think you are a girl with a very low type of mind. No dear, Mr. Sellers was a perfect gentleman and left me at my door with a kiss on the hand, and to make my Arabian Night adventure, as you call it, more incredible, I *actually* got the job.

Was it only a few days ago? I can hardly believe it. One by one the veils of illusion have been rudely torn from me leaving me weak and broken on the wheel of life. There is frenzy in my eyes, palsy in my hands, and a madness creeps in my being.

This is the first night I have reached home before midnight and only Marjorie Hillis and the need to express myself sustain me sufficiently to sit upright and unburden myself to you. For now I am really living alone and far from liking it, despite the fact I swallowed every word Miss Hillis had to say about the matter. Taking a leaf out of her book on what a lone girl does on an off-night, I bathed myself with some beautiful smelling salts, donned my best negligee (that tattered old number Aunt Agnes sent me years back), had my tray in bed (some limp lettuce and sardines) and am now sitting at my desk cradled in the warmth and light of a ghastly lamp, all fringe and pink silk.

Thursday was the day that really did me in.

It is *Der Tag!* The Boss is coming home.

I am sitting at my desk, cool but not composed, in my black linen dress with white collar and cuffs. There is a predatory gleam in my eyes—starch in my backbone for so far I have not met Mr. Brand and I must make good. You'd imagine the rest of the staff, the publicity boys, the production unit, might be taking it all as a matter of course. But no, from the moment I arrive in the morning, this lunatic asylum is berserk. It's Miss Lawrence, see that Brand gets this script first thing. Miss Lawrence, these set designs must be okayed as soon as Brand arrives. Miss Lawrence, there is an important meeting today to decide about the convention of Super Films salesmen. Miss Lawrence, have a heart and get me in there. I gotta see the chief about that cabaret scene. Miss Lawrence, tell the boss immediately that we can't find chairs that are authentic Russian barber-chairs. Maybe we had better switch it into a dentist's office. . . . Miss Lawrence this and Miss Lawrence that . . . I am going mad!

And to top it all, Mrs. B. calls me and wants me to find out why she didn't get that dress she ordered at Bullock's and will I please see to it that Sidney takes his pills a half hour after lunch every day and his nap and be sure and get those tickets for the opening of the Lunts tonight. . . .

"What am I," I yell at Jim Palmer, "a secretary or a mother's helper?" Jim is head of the Publicity Department.

"Woman's place is in the home," he says severely to me. "That's what you get for insisting on the vote."

"You're a big help," I blubber at him.

"Give me a little time," he grins at me. "In the meantime, however, Maggie, I have got to see the Great Man about a publicity tie-up with the Navy on the *Wings Over Hawaii* picture."

"Get out!" I scream at him.

By the time three o'clock arrives, the staff all has the jitters and they are sitting around like wooden soldiers and only an occasional shudder proves they are human.

"Why," I ask Jim, "do they all look so scared? You'd think Mussolini was arriving with a flock of black shirts."

"That's what's the matter with this lousy business," says Jim. "There's no security in it. At any minute, at any time, off go their heads and they are on the outside looking in. And it's a very cold place out there," he says, waving his hand toward the window. "You never know when you will eat again."

"You talk too much," says Maxine Stoddard. She is there, though why, I can't imagine, because she doesn't belong in our unit. She is a typist in the typing department. But after lunch she shows up with a bunch of flowers which she personally puts in a vase in S. B.'s room.

Jim gives her a sort of pitying look which makes Maxine flush, but he says nothing. I am reminded of some evil things I have heard about Maxine because it seems she gets too intimate with the bosses and I am suddenly very sorry for her and think perhaps I will be extra nice.

The time stretches on and by now I too become infected with this paralyzing fright and feel sure my knees will collapse. I am most annoyed at myself for being affected by all this and keep telling myself, "Don't be a sap, this is not a matter of life and death." But it is no use. The shine on my nose becomes worse. My fingers are cold, my palms clammy when up to the door rolls a stunning car and out rolls our liege lord.

I am rooted to the spot so that even when he makes his entrance greetings to Amanda and Buddy, I am still not able to make my way to him and introduce myself. He waves to the others, then lopes over to me. "Glad to have you with us," he mumbles. Somehow I manage to say my name and give him my clammy digits, at the same time gathering an impression of prominent eyes, thinning hair, flabby mouth and wide, feminine hips.

Then he is yelling orders at me in rapid fire succession. "Get me Cahan . . . tell him this . . . send for the manicurist . . . bring your book," and tops it with a request for something to eat. Something to eat? What? Oh, anything you think of and I'd like it soon—I'm famished. My first contact with this man and I'm supposed to know the state of his stomach and what he likes to feed on! Buddy comes to my rescue and dashes off to the commissary.

All this time Maxine has been standing off on the side waiting for a personal word with the boss. He seems to be avoiding her, though I remember what Buddy said about her expecting to have my job. I think it is very cruel of him, so I say something about the lovely flowers she brought for him.

"Oh," he says. "Thanks, Maxine. That was nice of you," and gives her an absent-minded paternal pat about the shoulders at the same time gently pushing her doorwards.

Buddy hops back with a ham on rye and a chocolate soda. I carry it into S. B.'s office feeling like a mother with a chick. Already plunged into a mass of papers on the desk, Mr. Brand reaches for the sandwich with an unseeing eye and tears into it, at the same time making a wild grope for the straw in the chocolate soda. I sit there with my book, and between bites and sips Mr. Brand answers phone calls and dictograph calls and dictates madly.

When the tray has been removed, our cutter, S. B.'s assistant, and a couple of writers burst in. S. B. tells me to transcribe what notes I have and wait until he can finish the rest of his dictation.

I gather myself together, catch my breath and sit at my machine in my own office. It is nearly six o'clock when I look up again and Amanda and Buddy are saying goodnight to me. Still no sign from Mr. Brand. Seven o'clock and I am waiting in solitary grandeur for Mr. Brand to come out and go home. For after all people do have places for which they pay rent and have wives and children to see—surely Mr. Brand is one of them. But no, time fugits on and Mr. Brand is busy creating escapes from realism for Mary and John Doe while I ponder upon the rumbling in my stomach and my fate.

Suddenly there is a strange buzzing in my ear. Now which one of the instruments can it be? After moving hectically all over the desk I decide to try the dictograph. Perhaps Mr. Brand is not in the coma I believe he is. Will I please make five highballs—sparkling water and not too much of that? Where, I ask myself, is the stuff with which to make these gigglefests? I search wildly about my office and even thumb a few panels hoping for a hidden cabinet but I have no luck. Finally in desperation I call in to Mr. Brand. I can't find the bar, I tell him. Oh, says he, it's in my office. The thought then strikes me that maybe Mr. Brand has hurt his leg and that all the other people have left and that he needs the five drinks to bolster himself, else why should he call me to come into his office to make drinks? But in I go and am barmaid for five very lazy, dissolute guys.

And while I am playing barmaid the phone rings and it is

Mrs. B. "I'm sorry, darling," her husband coos, "but I can't possibly make that opening tonight. But you go and take your mamma with you."

There are some high nervous screeches over the wire and Mr. B. holds the phone away from his ear.

"Yes, dear, I know. It's too bad—but I'll get home just as soon as I can. . . ."

I am thinking I need a drink, too, but no one asks me so I retreat into my own office and the hours draw on. I am faint with hunger and anger when Mr. Brand's door opens and he emerges with his pals, giving them last-minute instructions and saying to me he would now like to attack the mail. At that moment Mr. Brand is in danger of being attacked himself and I can even see the lovely lurid headlines, "Secretary Attacks Employer—Excuse Temporary Insanity Due To Malnutrition."

But no. I am a faithful creature and trot in dutifully behind Mr. Brand. The building is still as a tomb. Now, says Mr. Brand brightly, we can tear off a little work in peace. Firmly I make a quiet statement of the condition of my stomach. Mr. Brand is most contrite, asks why I didn't have something sent over and says he will try to get through with all the work quickly so I can leave for dinner.

Then for the first time Mr. Brand takes a real look at me. But from the controlled expression on his face I cannot get an idea of what he thinks. Perhaps I think that is the way I affect people. I am waiting for some comment but instead he calls for another drink. All the time I am mixing it I can feel his eyes boring into me. It makes me a little nervous.

However, when I give him the drink he becomes most businesslike and plunges into the mass of letters and papers on his desk. I struggle manfully to keep up with the flow of words. My pothooks become a little hectic and I will have to put my trust in my memory. A glimpse at my watch tells me it is eleven o'clock. When, oh, when will this man finish telling people off, telling people what to do, acknowledging notes and noting things? Perhaps my spirit of desperation reaches him because suddenly Mr. Brand stops and says, "To hell with this—we will tackle the rest tomorrow."

I gather my papers quickly before he can change his mind and get up, saying how nice it will be to take a quick look at a steak. Mr. Brand is now very cordial and asks how I like Hollywood and if I like working for him. I am woman enough to know how to respond to that, so I open my eyes wide and say I am just crazy about it, and working for him, and move over to the door.

Mr. Brand rises out of his chair and moves in my direction, all the time talking about the wonders of Hollywood and how he is sure I will make good because obviously I am very intelligent. I am about to open the door when I feel something moving over my back and I am stunned to discover it is Mr. Brand's arm and he pulls me around face to face with him.

I am so taken by surprise that I do not think very fast, but one thing I do know and that is I will not be thrust into the undignified position of having to fight for my honor. So I look him straight in the eye and I thank him for thinking I am intelligent and the most intelligent thing I can think of at this moment for me to do is to find myself some food and get my girlish sleep so I can be bright and intelligent again in the morning. I am sure, I continue in a motherly tone, that he is very tired, too, and tomorrow will be a big day for him.

There is a puzzled look in his eyes when I finish, but his arm slacks about me so I can breathe easily again.

"You are a very naïve girl," he says to me. "After all what's a kiss or two? Merely a friendly gesture."

There is no answer to that one without being unmaidenly

and one thing I am determined not to be is unmaidenly. So I say that I think perhaps I will always be naïve for I have discovered that it is more healthy.

There is a complete change in his attitude and I think maybe Mr. Brand gets my idea and decides that he too has had enough for one night but at the same time he would like to have the parting shot for he says paternally I shouldn't be so prim because he likes me. I am so different.

And I hope, I say, not to be outdone, that he is going to like me much better. However, there is nothing personal in my tone.

Love,
Maggie

4

Sinners in Asylum

SUPER FILMS

INTER-OFFICE COMMUNICATION

To: *Fred Cook* Subject: *Story For Sarya Tarn*
From: *Sidney Brand* Date: *November 6*

Must have story for Sarya Tarn's first American vehicle. We are spending a lot of money on her and only the best will do. I would suggest successful play or a best-selling novel. I expect synopses on my desk tomorrow. We *do not* want a career story; or an immigrant girl or anything too risqué. Miss Tarn speaks good English but with an accent so it will have to be a foreign part.

SB

SUPER FILMS
INTER-OFFICE COMMUNICATION

To: *James Palmer*   Subject: *Sarya Tarn*
From: *Sidney Brand*   Date: *November 6*

Have set deal with Sarya Tarn, famous European star, for exclusive contract with Super Films. Legal Department is drawing up contract. Check with them before you break story and then go to town! I've had some very satisfactory talks with Miss Tarn at Palm Springs and she is most agreeable to any sort of publicity so long as it is dignified. I'm sure Miss Tarn is going to be an important star. She has glamour, ability and what it takes. Miss Lawrence will arrange appointment for you to meet Miss Tarn.

SB

SUPER FILMS
INTER-OFFICE COMMUNICATION

To: *Madge Lawrence*   Subject: *Tarn*
From: *James Palmer*   Date: *November 6*

Dear Maggie:

At Mr. Brand's request, please arrange for me to see Tarn at the office tomorrow morning. I wouldn't mind having quote a few satisfactory talks unquote with her myself if she but remotely resembles some of the stills I have seen of her.

JP

SUPER FILMS
INTER-OFFICE COMMUNICATION

To: *Miss M. Lawrence* Subject: *Tarn Material*
From: *Fred Cook* Date: *November 6*

Dear Miss Lawrence:

I am checking my files for story suggestions but in the meantime am rushing you synopses of two plays and one best-selling novel, any one of which I think will be a knockout for Miss Tarn.

I would appreciate your seeing to it that Mr. Brand reads these at the earliest possible moment.

FC

FRANCES SMITH NOVEMBER 6
SUPER FILMS
NEW YORK CITY

STORY BREAKING TOMORROWS PAPERS SUPER ACQUISITION SARYA TARN OUR NEW FOREIGN STAR STOP ANXIOUS MAKE HER AMERICAN DEBUT IMPORTANT EXCITING AND PROFITABLE STOP WIRE ME ALL STORY SUGGESTIONS AND RUSH SYNOPSES IF WE DO NOT HAVE THEM AT COAST BY AIRMAIL SPECIAL DELIVERY REGARDS

SIDNEY BRAND

SUPER FILMS
INTER-OFFICE COMMUNICATION

To: *Miss Lawrence*   Subject: *Tarn*
From: *Fred Cook*   Date: *November 20*

Have not heard from Brand about any of the stories I sent in to him. Shall I keep on sending in more or has he changed his mind?

FC

SUPER FILMS
INTER-OFFICE COMMUNICATION

To: *Fred Cook*   Subject: *Tarn*
From: *Madge Lawrence*   Date: *November 20*

As you know, Mr. Brand has been in a whirl since his return from Palm Springs. I've written him a reminder note about the Tarn story suggestions and will speak with him further at the first possible opportunity. I will do everything I can to push this for you, but you know what I'm up against.

ML

SUPER FILMS
INTER-OFFICE COMMUNICATION

To: *Mr. Fred Cook*   Subject: *Guild play*
From: *Sidney Brand*   Date: *November 24*

I hear that Metro and Warners are bidding heavily for new Theatre Guild play. I hadn't even heard there was a Theatre Guild play. What in hell have I got a Scenario Department for?

SB

SUPER FILMS
INTER-OFFICE COMMUNICATION

To: *Miss M. Lawrence*   Subject: *Guild play*
From: *Fred Cook*   Date: *November 24*

I have dug into my files and find that I sent Mr. Brand a synopsis of the Guild play, *Sinners in Asylum*, not less than six months ago when I received a copy of the play from the author who is a friend of mine. I told him then re: communication of Feb. 4th that it looked like a smash hit. He said quote How in hell can you prove that? unquote. Well, it is proved now and unless my memory fails to serve me, that same synopsis is at this moment on his desk along with all the others.

FC

FRANCES SMITH   NOVEMBER 24

SUPER FILMS

NEW YORK CITY

AUTHORIZE YOU OFFER GUILD ONE HUNDRED AND FIFTY
THOUSAND DOLLARS FOR SINNERS IN ASYLUM STOP KEEP
ON BIDDING UNTIL YOU GET IT STOP REGARDS

SIDNEY BRAND

DAILY VARIETY

November 26

Sidney Brand of Super Films has acquired the new Guild
smash *Sinners in Asylum* for a reputed two hundred and forty-
five thousand dollars. It is to be the first starring vehicle for
Sarya Tarn the new Viennese importation.

STENOGRAPHER'S NOTEBOOK

Wire N. Y. get P. G. Wodehouse for adaptation *Sinners.*

Wire Frances Smith contact author *Sinners* come out Hollywood for adaptation six weeks guarantee $1,000 weekly, if
Wodehouse not available.

Send copies playscript to Research, Production, Wardrobe,
Casting and Art Departments.

Check with Palmer on why no banner line Carsons's column on *Sinners in Asylum* break.

Prepare list available writers and directors for SB re *Sinners*.

Have Casting prepare list casting suggestions.

ON BROADWAY
by Walter Winchell

November 27

What w.k. smart producer is having a tough time with the Hays office because of the race angle in that play that cost him a quarter of a million dollars? And the rumor is that he's burning because he didn't take time out to read it first. Tee hee!

SUPER FILMS
INTER-OFFICE COMMUNICATION

To: *Madge Lawrence*   Subject: *La Tarn*
From: *James Palmer*   Date: *November 27*

Dear Maggie:

Am having terrible time with Sarya Tarn. Her English is not as good as it was in Palm Springs and besides Tarn not knowing who Stella Carsons was made a lifelong enemy by referring to her as "that fat peasant." And besides all editors are fed up on foreign importations. I'm afraid S. B. will have to dig down and pay for space if he wants it. He's digging for everything else. Why should Publicity be a step-child?

How about dinner tonight?

J.

SUPER FILMS
INTER-OFFICE COMMUNICATION

To: *Jim Palmer*   Subject: *Food*
From: *Madge Lawrence*   Date: *November 27*

What is dinner? I can faintly remember way back in the dim past of sitting down at a table at seven o'clock and having minions fly around trying to entice my appetite. But that's all a lost dream. I now take a cheese on rye whenever and if ever I get it. Tonight, my friend, I am to take Miss Tarn's pooch to the vet. She can't trust it to a mere servant. So what does that make me?

Thanks anyway, but what has happened to all those artists' models you used to feed?

ML

P.S. However, you may feed me on Thanksgiving.

WESTERN UNION

SIDNEY BRAND   DECEMBER 1
SUPER FILMS
HOLLYWOOD CALIFORNIA

WODEHOUSE ON VACATION IN ENGLAND STOP NEITHER
TEARS NOR MONEY WILL ENTICE HIM STOP JOHN TUS-
SLER AUTHOR SINNERS VERY KEEN ON HOLLYWOOD
STOP WILL COME FOR TWO THOUSAND A WEEK ON
THREE MONTHS TERMER STOP SHALL I CLOSE DEAL

STOP TUSSLER NOW RATED AMONG THREE GREAT LIVING
AMERICAN PLAYWRIGHTS STOP METRO WOULD PAY HIM
MORE BUT ANXIOUS WORK ON HIS OWN PLAY REGARDS
FRANCES SMITH

ON BROADWAY
by Walter Winchell

December 1

The Hays office and Super Films have finally come out of their huddle on *Sinners in Asylum.* The play, a Theatre Guild smash, was purchased by Super for a paltry quarter of a million. Dollars my dear public! It concerns the very sensational theme of a mulatto girl and a white man. But that's all fixed now. *They are making her Spanish!*

WESTERN UNION

SIDNEY BRAND   DECEMBER 1
SUPER FILMS
HOLLYWOOD CALIFORNIA

WHAT DO YOU MEAN YOU ARE MAKING HER SPANISH
STOP THE WHOLE POINT OF THE PLAY WILL BE LOST STOP
I WILL NOT BE PARTY TO ANY SUCH COMMERCIALISM
STOP MY PLAY GOES ON AS IS OR ELSE
JOHN TUSSLER

WESTERN UNION

JOHN TUSSLER   DECEMBER 1

THEATRE GUILD

NEW YORK CITY

IS IT MY FAULT IF HAYS OFFICE WON'T LET ME BE ARTIS-
TIC STOP FOR TWO THOUSAND WEEKLY YOU SHOULD BE
WILLING SERVE AS PALLBEARER AT YOUR OWN FUNERAL
STOP EXPECT YOU SOON STOP BEST WISHES

                          SIDNEY BRAND

December 1

Dear Liz:

Your alarm unnecessary. No, the villain did not hurl me out into the cold snow because I didn't let him have his way with me, but instead he has taken a permanent option on my every waking moment which in his language is twenty-four hours out of the day.

You see, darling, and doubtless you have seen by the daily papers, that we have a new foreign star and while you and the rest of the laity palpitate in expectation of the lady's debut, I am busy working to make it a fact. Give me none of your hollow laughs. I am fully aware of the fact that I am just an office slavey but in my spare moments (and they are definitely spare), I dabble in such quaint pastimes as finding a house that will suit Miss Tarn, servants who can cook her pet Viennese dishes, a maid who can put her to bed, the right kind of vet for her dog, a hairdresser whose artistic aura is akin to her own, a couturier who will cover the fact that she is a trifle bow-legged and too short in the legs.

To add to all this, Mr. Brand has done me the honor of making me his personal valet. I mix his drinks, lay out his evening clothes, put studs in his shirts, but on the other eve I was properly floored when he asked me to fix his shaving lather while he talked to New York on long distance phone.

Picture me if you can in the black and white tile bathroom off his office dreamily stirring hot water into the shaving mug. Outside the stars are overhead, a dizzy moon hangs low, the scented air gently stirs the white frilled cellophane curtains and other girls are actually sitting out dances, carelessly sipping cocktails, unheeding of the workaday night while I am spending my romantic soul in raising a lather. Incidentally, considering it's my initial effort, I do a very fine job.

My liege lord, after $60 worth of telling off a poor unsuspecting advertising man what *He* would have done if *He* had anything to do with *These* layouts, enters the bathroom. I hand him his lather and razor and start to leave as any nice girl would, but no, he hands me a script and waving me to sit on the bath stool, says, "Be a good girl, Madge, and read me this play while I shave. We're having a story conference at my house at ten tomorrow morning and I won't have a chance to read this tonight because I've got to go to an anniversary dinner for my mother-in-law." And would you believe it, the script is *Sinners in Asylum* for which we have paid a quarter of a million dollars and Winchell was right.

Half an act later my boss says, "That's swell, Madge, you've got a good reading voice. Now I'd better hurry. Call up my wife and tell her I'm on my way."

I heave a heavy sigh of relief and Mr. Brand says suddenly, "What do you do with your private life?" I say to him, "Mr.

Brand, you talk about it as though it was a pill that you took a half an hour after eating. I wish to God it was so, because can you tell me when I could have a private life?"

I think that will hold him. But he laughs a gay, mocking laugh and tosses off an unusually good epigram. "Still waters," says he, "run deep."

What do you think?

Love,
Maggie

5

I Become a Female Angle

Dear Aunt Agnes:

It is very difficult to explain to you why I really haven't time to write oftener. Even this tidbit comes your way only because Mr. Brand went back to sleep after breakfast.

You see, we were all due here at his house this morning at ten o'clock for a story conference. Yes, I know it's Sunday but we are rushed for time for a story to launch that new foreign actress, Sarya Tarn, you have been reading about. I arrived here at ten sharp along with the director, Monk Faye; Mr. Brand's assistant, Roy Tyson; the author of the play, John Tussler; and Philip Skinner, one of our best scenario writers.

I do wish you could see Mr. Brand's house. It is a sprawling California hacienda filled with French Provincial furniture and a mob of elegant English servants careening around, to say nothing of tennis courts, swimming pool and a model farm. It's all very feudal.

Well, as I say, we all arrived at ten and the butler told us Mr. Brand did get up and dress and eat his breakfast but then decided to go to sleep again. So, that gave me a chance to write you.

Mr. Faye is most annoyed and is saying some very cutting things about Mr. Brand; Mr. Tyson is playing solitaire; Mr. Tussler, who just arrived from New York this morning, stares at us as though we were inside cages; and Mr. Skinner, who has been in Hollywood a long time, is taking time out for a quiet nap.

This is the first time I have been invited to attend a story conference and I am very excited about it. Mr. Brand told me that I am to take down in shorthand everything that is said in the conference so that nothing valuable will be lost.

Mr. Skinner just awakened out of his nap and is telling about a wonderful dream that he had. I can't hear much of what he is saying but it must be most amusing, because even Mr. Tussler awakes out of his lethargy and says he can swap an even better one. And it is—for they all laugh very loudly.

Then a pretty little French maid on very high heels trips into the room and says, "Sh! Sh!" She then whispers to Mr. Faye and he nods. After she leaves, he tells us that we must be very quiet as Mrs. Brand is going to have a baby soon and is not feeling well.

Now it is one o'clock and we are all very hungry, and still no Mr. Brand. Mr. Faye summons the butler and asks him to find out when Mr. Brand will be with us. We fidget and fidget and then the butler returns and says that Mr. Brand will be right down.

Mr. Brand has just come in.

"It's lunch time," growls Mr. Faye.

"Oh, that's all right," says Mr. Brand. "I've had a tray in my room. Let's get going."

So now I will have to say good-bye and my love to you.

Madge

STENOGRAPHER'S NOTEBOOK

BRAND: Glad to see you here with us, Tussler. Did you have a nice trip out? Where are you staying?

TUSSLER: Yes. I'm . . .

BRAND: Say, Monk. How much did you drop at the Clover Club last night?

FAYE: I came out ahead. How about you?

BRAND: They took me for plenty. I can't win. Tussler, we're going to do big things with that play of yours. Super is selling the rest of its product on the strength of it. We've got to put it over. It'll cost a million before we get on the set. You're a highway robber, Tussler, but the joke's on you. The Government will take most of it.

SKINNER: He won't mind that. He's a member of the Communist Party.

BRAND: A communist! Why didn't somebody tell me? Don't I have enough trouble?

TUSSLER: But, Mr. Brand. I'm not. . . .

BRAND: All right . . . all right, Tussler. You're safe enough with me. I'm no red-baiter. Just so long as you don't start a revolution at Super!

TUSSLER: But, Mr. Brand, *I'm not* . . .

BRAND: Let's get down to business or *I'll* start a revolution. Madge, be sure and get every word we say! Now boys, the important thing is to stick as closely as possible to the original play. After all, there are a lot of people in New York who paid good money to see this play, so it must have something. But, of course, we have to remember the Hays office. I have been sweating for days, I give you my word, to put this thing over with them and it was only after I gave them my solemn word of honor that I would handle this with my usual good taste, finesse and delicacy that they said to me OK Brand, we trust you to do the right thing. Now boys, I can't let them down and you can't let me down!

TYSON: You know us, Chief. We've never let you down yet.

BRAND: Thanks, Roy. And another thing. I've promised the Hays office to change the title. You see *Sinners in Asylum* is connected in the public mind with a very unsavory theme. Sure, we're changing the theme but that's not enough. We have to wipe out in the public consciousness all connection with *Sinners in Asylum.*

TUSSLER: But why . . .

BRAND: Now, Monk. I've never told you yet how to shoot a picture. *I'm* paying *you* to do that but this time things are different. I want you to do the best you can for Sarya Tarn but don't burn up the film by giving me fifty-seven takes of a scene. I don't need fifty-seven takes to know what's good. I've got an instinct for those things.

TYSON: You bet you have, Chief.

BRAND: Thanks, Roy. And also, Monk, see if you can't forget that creepy tempo you gave me the last time. The hell with your artistic camera angles. We've got something to sell this time—Sarya Tarn!

TUSSLER: But, my pl——

FAYE: All right, Sidney. I'll tell you what. You go out on the set and I'll sit in your office and we'll see what you can do with that dame. It would be a pleasure!

BRAND: What are you getting sore about? Now you, Skinner, we're paying Tussler a fortune to write this adaptation. All right, so he's one of the three greatest American playwrights. But has he ever written for the screen? What are his credits?

None! But you—you know what it's all about and I'm depending on you to see to it that we get the finest screenplay of the year. You never know, we might even get the Academy Award.

TYSON: You're due for one, Chief. That was a lousy deal you got last year.

BRAND: You're right. Thanks, Roy. Madge, you're sure you're getting everything?

ME: Yes, Mr. Brand.

SKINNER: Say, Chief. Who are you going to get to play opposite Tarn? It's very important because until I know who the leading actors are I can't get the right feel of the script.

TUSSLER: But—what's the diff——

BRAND: Don't worry. I'm negotiating right now for Gable!

TYSON: Gee, Chief, that's perfect!

BRAND: Thanks, Roy. Now, Phil, this is a suggestion, but bear it in mind while you're writing. It's just what I'd like. Tarn's got to be a sympathetic character. This is the first time she's being presented to the American public. Now, the dame in the play is not sympathetic enough, so we've got to make Tarn more naïve. And it's right that she should be naïve. Here is this girl who has lived all her life on an island off the African coast.

TUSSLER: But it isn't in Afr——

BRAND: She has never known a mother's love and her old man, this Swedish sea-captain, was killed with her mother when she was a baby. The only love she has known is from animals and the kindly natives of the village. So she is naïve—but on the inside there is a roaring volcano . . . her mother's Spanish blood!

SKINNER: I get what you mean, Chief. I get it . . .

BRAND: Here in this primitive background, Monk, I'll let you have your camera angles. I want production value here. Later on it's another story.

Tyson: Say, Chief, maybe we can save some dough here by picking up stock film from *Bring 'Em Back Alive.*

Brand: Thanks, Roy. Hey, wait a minute. What do you mean? Will you climb out of your quickie background! This is a major studio production. But on the other hand, it might not be a bad idea. See what you can pick up, Roy.

Faye: Listen, Sidney. I hate to disagree with you because I know you're all excited. But I don't see where Tarn has the fire for this role.

Brand: Never mind, Monk. You leave that to me. I'll see to it that she gives you plenty of fire. Boy, I can just see her when all the Spanish in her breaks loose. She's a hell cat! Like an animal she scratches back when she comes face to face with an artificial civilization. She's got to be tamed! She's a wild thing with bars around her. She's caged! My God! What a title! *Lady in a Cage!*

Tyson: Gosh, what a title!

Brand: Thanks, Roy. Can you see it on the twenty-four sheets . . . on the marquee . . . SUPER FILMS IS PROUD TO INTRODUCE SARYA TARN IN THE SEASON'S MOST ASTOUNDING DRAMA—*Lady in a Cage.*

Faye: I don't care what you call it. I just thought of an angle on the love interest that is terrific! Here you have a dame . . . living in an outpost of civilization . . . she's beautiful . . . she's luscious . . . she's untouched! She's everything to drive a man crazy. She's grown up wild in the jungle. Now this is my idea. There's a shipwreck and Gable is washed up on the shore. He wakes up to see this gorgeous creature looking down at him. There's a passion flower in her hair. That's symbolic. He stares at her . . . unbelieving. . . . She runs away . . . frightened. . . . He follows . . . the animal in him aroused.

Tussler: But—!

Brand: Wait a minute, Monk. She wouldn't run away. She

wouldn't be afraid. Remember, she may be naïve, untouched, but inside of her is this flame . . . this Spanish blood. . . . She would be too fascinated to run.

SKINNER: Listen. I know a thing or two about dames. I've had a thousand of 'em. This dame . . .

BRAND: Why should we argue about female psychology when there is a woman in the room. Monk, you ask Madge what she would do. Now Madge, listen carefully.

FAYE: We take the camera over to a close-up of Gable's face. It is moonlight. We have a long shot of this jungle and the jungle moon hanging low. Into the camera comes Sarya Tarn, chanting a native love song. She is the spirit of the jungle night. The camera follows her as she dances into the waves—a wild thing! Suddenly she sees something . . . stops . . . the camera follows her and in a beautiful two-shot we see Sarya Tarn looking down at Gable's face. He opens his eyes. He thinks he is in a dream. Blindly he puts up his hand to . . . touch . . . to feel . . . It's flesh . . . warm, alive . . . He leaps to his feet . . . the camera moves back for a close two-shot of these two looking into each other's eyes, discovering each other. Mind you, Gable is the first white man Tarn has ever seen! All the dormant woman in her comes to life . . . He makes a grab for her. . . . She . . . Now, Miss Lawrence . . . if you were that girl . . . if you were there on that tropical beach with Gable, what would you do?

ME: I—

BRAND: Remember she's Spanish!

ME: I—

SKINNER: Her first white man!

TYSON: Gable!

ME: Well, I—

FAYE: Go on! Go on!

ME: Well—I should give in!

BRAND: What did I tell you? That proves my point.

TYSON: It's her Spanish blood, boss.

BRAND: You're telling me? Well, boys, that's enough for today. We've gone a long way and Tussler, it's been great having you here. You were invaluable and at the rate we're going we're bound to have a gorgeous script. See you all tomorrow at the studio. Have a pleasant week-end. . . .

6

It's Wonderful to Be a Mother

Dear Liz:

I have just become a mother so if you ever have a relapse and decide you are fed up on being an independent woman of the world and think that you need the little patter of feet to make you complete, harken to me.

It is a great joy but it is all very expensive. You begin payment from the moment you start losing your figure. Once however you have passed through this trying ordeal, the real payoff commences. The attending physician will guarantee to bring little Oscar into the world for not a cent under $2,000. But there are consultants. These are very superior gentlemen who go into conference with your own physician and corroborate his testimony that you are really going to have a baby. That costs $50 a visit. The suite at the hospital is a mere $35 a day. There are also nurses, day and night ones, and a little thing called extras which usually becomes the main item on your bill.

Now we come to the layette. If you have a lot of relatives, it is fairly simple but since you are supporting most of them you buy your own layette. This layette consists of all sorts of dresses and didies (monogrammed) and cummerbunds and whatnots, to say nothing of a beautiful English bassinet all upholstered in satin with fleecy tidbits to cover. All in all you can't get out under a round thousand even though your baby will grow out of these in a few months.

Then there is a nursery. Oh, I know you and I didn't have one when we were toddlers, but have you ever fully considered the importance of sunshine to a growing child? Just tossing it out into the back yard isn't going to help because it might get sunstroke or a variety of germs. So you summon a flock of architects to draw you some designs for a nursery all encased in a special infra-ray glass that will let in the good rays and keep out the evil ones. If you are lucky, you will pick the architect who has a sister-in-law who knows she would be a wow in pictures so instead of charging you the usual cost plus ten per cent plus anything else he can collect, he will just charge you a paltry five grand and guarantee that your child will have the most modern, up-to-date, germ-proof, fun-proof and burglar-proof mausoleum. Of course, there is a starched femme who must come home with little Oscar and is very costly and haughty and won't let you near him for fear of contamination. Sometimes the awful thought strikes me that it is pure dumb luck that you and I are still alive and apparently in possession of most of our faculties.

Six A.M. this morning I am routed out of my bed and rushed to the hospital in order to hold Mr. Brand's hand. It seems he is disconsolate what with the hospital staff in Mrs. Brand's room and nobody around to cheer him.

For a quiet half hour I sit beside Mr. Brand and permit him to clutch my arm, while doctors and nurses flit past us with very grave faces, relaxing only occasionally to give the anxious father an indulgent smile or two. But little Oscar after the first fright reneges, probably chuckling to himself that already he has put one over on the old man.

Everyone relaxes in general now with the exception of Mr. Brand who proceeds to have a nervous collapse and yells hoarsely for an M.D. A sedative is administered to him by the chief of staff himself and after a gurgle or two and a flutter of his eyelids, he decides to live. This makes for a nice pause so that Dr. X can engage Mr. Brand in conversation and ask him why it is that producers are all the time making medical pictures that are not authentic? Now he can tell Mr. Brand some stories about experiences he has had that would make the most marvelous pictures. Someday he says he will maybe take time off to do just that little thing, dash off a story or two just to show the industry. He knows he can write for he has published quite a lot of stuff already in the medical journals.

Mr. Brand wears a strained expression something like a man who has just come out from under fire and is trying to readjust himself to normal life once more but doesn't quite contact. He doesn't appear to hear what the doctor is saying, which perhaps is just as well because he might become violent. I stare at my somnambulent boss and become perturbed. Maybe he will not come out of this coma. I recall cases of shell shock and remember that cures have been effected by rousing the patient through further shock. I toy with the idea of taking desperate measures and ponder on going into a cataleptic fit myself.

Then like a sleepwalker awakening, Mr. Brand shudders. He makes a few pathetic passes with a limp hand over his face. Is it possible, I think, that this man can really be deeply affected like other normal human beings by the primitive forces of life?

Then bingo! The Brand body shakes itself into reality and we are off! "Get me Wardrobe! Call off my luncheon appointment with Tarn; get me Cahan on long distance; find a room here where I can work; find a room where you can work (meaning me) get a room where Tussler and Skinner can work. I want them here!" I do not stop to question him. I do not say, "Mr. Brand, this is a hospital and not a hotel." I fly. For it seems that not only am I to cooperate in having Mr. Brand's baby, but I also must assist in keeping the wheels of production humming so that Sarya Tarn, like Oscar, can be launched. I am at the door when he yells, ". . . and have Palmer here ready to send out announcements to the papers about the baby!" So you can see he still remembers that he is going to become a father.

I hie me to the business office. I want some rooms, I say, nice quiet rooms where our production staff can operate. The business office looks at me peculiarly. Now, now, they calm me. You don't need a lot of rooms. All you need is a nice quiet bed and we can fix you up very comfortably in the ward. I see they think I am a mental case. I explain who I am and why we have to have some rooms. The words "Brand" and "pictures" are magic. Unfortunately, however, it seems the hospital is full of a lot of patients. There is a lady in maternity, though, who will be leaving shortly and Mr. Brand can have her room. In the meantime we will have to use the solarium. It is pleasant and sunny up there. I put in some calls for the studio and report back to S. B.

He is in a complaining mood. He doesn't like the way the hospital is run. The floors are slippery. Why don't they have carpets? What if a nurse fell while carrying an infant?

I quietly point out to him that hospitals must be antiseptic and that rugs are nice warm breeding places for germs.

I think it is a good point. He thinks they could do something about it.

I search for an antidote and hit upon the brilliant idea that

62   JANE ALLEN

he may be hungry. How about some breakfast? He brightens.
So I telephone the kitchen and they are very cordial and say
they will send up a tray immediately.

While we wait I take down a few letters and complaints.
When an orderly comes in with a tray, I give one sniff and feel
faint myself for it is full of appetizing ham and eggs. But Mr.
Brand doesn't react favorably. He sneers. He can't eat that stuff.
Call the Brown Derby, he yells at me, and have them send up
a mushroom omelette. Remember to tell them it's for Brand.
What about this tray? I ask. Oh, you can have it, says Mr.
Brand. So I do.

I have barely finished my repast when a wild-eyed orderly
bursts in. The telephone girl, he says, is going berserk. It seems
that everyone at Super Films is on the phone all at once trying
to get hold of Mr. Brand and they all say it is a matter of life
and death.

"Can't a man have a baby in peace?" howls Mr. Brand.

But it seems he can't for there are a lot of other people who
have babies and people who are ill and their friends have phones
and would like to know how they are so the switchboard can't
all the time be answering calls for Mr. Brand. The orderly
explains all this just as politely as he can. "My God," groans
Mr. Brand. "Do I have to worry about that too? Get another
switchboard," he roars. "Get another telephone girl."

So it is up to me to take the orderly by the hand and lead
him to the switchboard where we all go into a huddle. We have
about completed negotiations when I sense an alien atmosphere
in the room and look up to find Jim Palmer.

"Hello, toots," he says vulgarly.

I am very pleased to see him, for somehow even if Jim Palmer
is a screwball he has a soothing effect on me.

No, my dove, it is not an amorous feeling he evokes. On the contrary. He is to me what a prairie oyster is to you after a big night—exotic to the taste, but very clarifying to the mind.

"I am certainly glad to see you," I say with the utmost cordiality.

"This is a break," he says. "It must be that hospitals have a sentimental effect on you. How about dinner with me tonight in the emergency ward?"

"That will be very cozy," I say, "for doubtless unless little Oscar chooses to make his debut shortly, we are going to take a long-term option on this hospital."

"So," he snorts, "little Oscar is holding up production, is he? That must be a blow to Brand. Hasn't he asked you to do something about it, Maggie?"

"Darling," I say sweetly, "I'd have the baby myself if I could to end this suspense, but in the meantime we had better present ourselves to the great man . . ."

"Yeah, before he signs up all the nurses on the maternity floor."

In the solarium an old man in a wheel chair is fretting to his nurse, but otherwise the place is deserted. We make inquiries of the nurse but she says she hasn't seen Mr. Brand at all.

It occurs to me that perhaps he has been summoned to his wife's room for the announcement of the main event, but all is quiet and serene there and inquiries to the floor nurse elicit no information.

We make a grand tour of the hospital. We duck in and out of rooms; we dodge stretcher beds; wheel chairs, ether machines. All we gather in our wake are muttered imprecations and a load of anesthetics which are suffocating. There is nothing for it but to make our way back to the solarium.

There we find Messrs. Tussler and Skinner. The former is looking more dazed than ever. Why, he queries, is his presence necessary because Mr. Brand is going to have a baby?

"Relax, relax," Skinner jeers at him, "and give yourself an eyeful of the girls in white. There was a honey that just came by with red hair. I'll bet she knows why she was created and for what."

"You must be patient, Skinner," Jim withers him. "Tussler has hardly been with us long enough to discover that we not only preoccupy ourselves with sex at the box office but feel we must live life as we see it on the screen for twenty-four hours a day."

"Aw hell," says Skinner. "Even a comrade takes time out for sex."

"For the last time," cries Tussler. "I'm not . . ."

"Hy-yah, folks!"

It is Rawley of the Art Department carrying a big folder of sketches. "Where's the boss? Has the infant arrived? What goes on?"

"Make yourself at home," Jim invites. "This is a nice place to get the sun. Order up a chair and a drink and, Skinner permitting, you might get a pretty little nurse to hold your hand."

"Swell! Bring on your nurses."

The phone rings. I answer it. It is switchboard and she wants to know where S. B. is. Long distance is ready from New York besides a flock of other calls from the studio and, switchboard coos to me, "Do you know that Miss Tarn just called to ask about Mrs. Brand and she was the sweetest thing!"

I muffle switchboard with a few curt orders to trace Mr. Brand in the hospital.

Switchboard is more than willing. She can already envision herself ravishing an army of cameras with her profile.

"The only thing that's got her down," I tell Jim, "is that she wishes she had worn her best blue instead of that old brown thing."

"Hollywood is a wonderful place," he says dourly.

And now Eric of Wardrobe is upon us waving a group of sketches.

"Don't you think, Mr. Tussler, this would be divine for Miss Tarn in that first sequence? It covers just enough of her to leave everything to the imagination."

"Hello, Madge," he yoo-hoos at me, "has the little chap arrived yet?"

"No! And the big chap has disappeared," I say snappishly.

"Yo—ho! Here we come!" Props . . . and three of them are crowding into the solarium carrying wigs, weapons and some jungle decorations.

"This is just dandy," cracks Jim. "Now we can settle ourselves to shooting the picture."

"Yeah, and where's the script?"

Roy Tyson is upon us. All we need now is Sarya and a few cameras and everything would be perfect.

"Whatdoyoumean the script?" Skinner squares off—and the battle is on—yam-yamming about what the hell does Brand expect and they are already on the fourth sequence and who in hell can turn out an Academy winner in a week.

Switchboard rings back to say she cannot locate Mr. Brand but is doing everything she can and in the meantime, will I take a few calls. I hang onto the phone for twenty minutes and finally get hold of Bud and implore him to see that no more studio calls come through to us at the hospital unless it is *really important*!

"Okay," says Bud. "I've got everything under control."

I can tell by the tone of his voice that he is in Mr. Brand's office, his legs on the desk, playing his favorite game of movie executive.

It is way past lunch time when I get away from the phone and everyone is howling for food. I telephone for a flock of sandwiches and coffee and by now am in my usual limp condition.

Jim is sympathetic. "Let's duck out of this racket," he says, "and find a quiet place at the drugstore where we can have our lunch in peace."

I am very grateful to him and about to leave when switchboard rings. Mr. Brand is in Room 3B on the maternity floor and we are all to report there immediately.

There is a concerted rush to the door. We all push out into the corridor. Props drops a few spears; Tyson lets fly a manuscript; and when we make the elevator, crash goes Skinner's typewriter. He stops to pick it up while we pile into the elevator. "Hey," yells Skinner. "Wait for Baby!"

A nurse comes storming out.

"What is going on around here?" she asks grimly. "Who are you people and what are you doing here?"

Unfortunately she is neither young nor pretty, so Skinner does a casual, insolent take and shakes his head.

"Sorry, sister, but I'm busy every night."

She does a slow burn but before she can answer there is an insistent buzz of the elevator bell and we shoot downward.

We emerge on the third floor to face an elderly and very irate nurse.

"I'm the superintendent," she advises us crisply, "and I must ask you people to remember that this is a hospital and not a motion picture studio. You've managed to disregard that fact so far to say nothing of insulting the nurse on the solarium floor and turning the place into a bedlam. Mr. Brand is in the second room on the first left hand turning. Now let's see how quiet you can be in getting there. There are babies on this floor and very sick women."

Even Skinner manages to subside at this, though when we turn in on the left he makes a very rude noise.

The door of Mr. Brand's room is open and we all crowd in to gape at a singular spectacle.

Mr. Brand, looking very droll, is in bed with a clothespin on his nose. In his mouth is a sort of a funnel and a nurse stands by smiling encouragingly at him.

"Gee, are you sick, Chief?" asks Tyson feelingly.

S. B. makes vague gestures toward the clothespin and the funnel indicating he cannot answer.

"Who's having this baby anyway?" asks Skinner.

"Mr. Brand is having a basal metabolism taken," explains the nurse.

S. B. nods vigorously.

"I always say," says Skinner, "that there's nothing like a little basal metabolism taken twice a day."

Mr. Brand shakes his head violently.

"Hello, everybody!" Monk Faye pushes his way through to the bed and takes in the quaint tableau, especially the nurse.

"When do we test her, Brand?" he grins.

S. B. starts to shake his head again. The nurse removes the pin and the funnel.

"Whatthehell . . ." blusters Mr. Brand. "Can't a guy be sick without a lot of cheap wisecracks? My doctor has been advising me for months to have my basal metabolism taken and as long as I had to stay here anyway I thought it was a good time to do it. But would I get any sympathy? No! When do I have time to get away from the studio and take care of myself? What would happen if I did? I suppose if I dropped dead all you'd say is, 'Poor Brand. It's too bad he had to work so hard.'"

"Gee, boss . . . the studio would go pfff . . . without you," soothes Roy.

"Thanks, Roy."

I notice that the tray from the Brown Derby is by his bed untouched. I comment on this and Mr. Brand says they wouldn't let him eat before he made the test. However, that reminds him he is hungry as a bear, so would I please telephone the Brown Derby and have a filet mignon sent up and some apple strudel? I do.

The nurse procures some chairs; props Mr. Brand up with extra pillows and lopes out of the room with a studied angular stride. I have seen that lope somewhere before and suddenly remember it is peculiar to Katharine Hepburn.

"Mr. Brand . . . Mr. Brand." It is Eric waving frantically. "I've simply got to get an okay on these sketches and get back to the studio."

"All right, Eric. Let's see them."

Eric flits over to the bed and spreads out his portfolio.

S. B. turns over the pages carelessly but his eyes are wandering doorwards. For some curious reason there are a prodigious number of nurses strutting by in eccentric attitudes. Some of them remind you of Garbo or maybe it's Crawford. However, it must be legitimate because most of them are carrying babies, hypos or bedpans. It is all a little distracting, particularly to Mr. Brand.

"No . . . I don't like 'em," says Mr. Brand.

"I think they're honeys," enthuses Skinner.

"Keep it clean," says Mr. Brand. "I'm talking about the sketches. . . . Look, Eric, she's too dressed up for this sequence. I can't draw a line. I admit it. But I've seen pictures before and you can't tell me that a dame in the jungle is going to wear a Chanel creation. . . ."

"But Mr. Brand, this is exotic . . . this is exciting. You know perfectly well that illusion can be preserved only by covering

the form." Here Eric makes a few passes down his own divine
form.

"It all comes down to this, Eric. I want every woman in the
audience to itch to be in the jungle with nothing on like Tarn
and I want every man to get hot."

"In other words, Eric," breaks in Jim, "Mr. Brand wants you
to raise a wholesale libido!"

"That's a swell word, Jim, libido. That's just what I mean.
That's just what I want. It's up to you to give it to me. You'll
have plenty of time in the American sequence to do a Schiapa-
relli."

"But there are fashions even in the jungle, Mr. Brand. A
woman is a woman no matter what or where . . ."

"Okay, Eric, just so long as you keep everyone conscious of
the fact that she is a woman I'll be satisfied. But to hell with
illusions."

Eric appears injured.

"But, Mr. Brand . . ." he starts.

"Good-bye, Eric," says the boss. "Madge, telephone the doctor and see how Mrs. Brand is."

Eric shrugs his shoulders eloquently but gathers up his
sketches and departs. I am at the phone learning that all is
quiet on the maternal front.

"All right, Rawley, what have you got?"

Rawley spreads his layouts over the bed.

"Here's the jungle set. It's going to run a little over budget
but you told me to go to town. . . ."

"What do you mean by a little bit, Rawley?"

"Well, you see, boss, a good deal depends on where we go
for location."

"Say, Monk, haven't you picked out a location yet?"

"I was in the projection room all day yesterday looking over some film the boys brought back and I would say that Ensenada's the best bet."

"But, Monk, it'll cost a fortune down there."

"Yeah, but it'll be worth it. It's just what we want."

"But, Mr. Faye," says Roy, "you remember you said last night that Catalina would be fine. You know, over by the Isthmus."

"Well, why not, Monk? Certainly it would be cheaper."

"It's all the same to me but I like the fishing better at Ensenada," says Faye.

"That's just dandy, but we're not selling fish. We're selling motion pictures. Roy, you see the production office and make arrangements. In the meantime when I get back to the studio, I'll look at the film and let you know whether to go ahead on the Catalina location. Rawley, I'll okay these sketches if we go to Catalina but you had better make some additional layouts and cut costs in case we have to go to Ensenada—for Monk's fishing."

Props have pushed forward now, all decked in wigs and head-dresses and spears.

"What the hell is all this?" asks the boss.

"We want to get your okay. It's costing money to keep the stuff at the studio while we're waiting for it."

Mr. Brand looks over props casually.

"It looks okay to me. Okay."

"How long do you think you'll be tied up here, boss?" asks Roy.

The boss is suddenly metamorphosed into a father and sighs heavily.

"You cannot tell about these things, Roy, and I ought to stay around for Selma's sake at such a time."

"Well, do you want me to stick around?" asks Roy.

"Thanks, Roy, but you'd better get back to the studio. I'll keep

Tussler, Skinner and Monk here. Maybe we can get some script. It's nice and quiet here. Hey, Roy, get the name of that nurse who just passed by. She looks good to me. Maybe we'll test her."

"Okay, Chief," and the stooge bounds off followed by Rawley and props.

"Well, Skinner, how goes the script?"

"We've broken down the story line and are all set to go into dialogue."

"That's just fine," says Mr. Brand with heavy sarcasm. "You've got a story line and I've got my cameras all ready to shoot. What the hell are they going to shoot—a story line? I want dialogue. Is that too much to ask?"

"Now listen . . ." breaks in Skinner.

"Excuse me, please. Jim, have you written the announcements for the baby yet?"

"No . . . but I've got a rough idea of what might do," says Jim drily.

"Okay. While we're talking story you scribble some stuff and leave a blank space for the sex of the child."

"What—is there any doubt about it?" asks Jim innocently.

Mr. Brand ignores him.

"Listen, Skinner, I know I'm rushing you and you haven't had much time but they rush me all the time every day of the week. But I get my work done. Why can't you?"

"Well, look, boss. If you'd given me an experienced collaborator I would have had something. But I'm like a prep school for this guy. Not only do I have to write the story but I have to be a teacher. He wants art and I want an Academy winner and you can't mix oil and water."

"Look, Tussler," Mr. Brand pleads. "We're in this business to make money. You've got to stop being an intellectual and we'll show you how to write motion pictures."

"If it's all the same to you . . ." starts Mr. Tussler. He is looking very fierce.

"Madge, check about the baby," breaks in Mr. Brand.

I am glad for the interruption, as I have been experiencing some difficulty keeping a straight face because of Jim who is hunched over in his chair like the statue of the Thinker with wrinkled brows, sucking a pencil, and apparently drawing upon all his genius to think up something brilliant to say about Mr. Brand's baby.

"How about this, Mr. Brand . . ." he says. "A blank was born to Mrs. Selma Brand, wife of the eminent producer, Sidney Brand of Super Films. Mother and child are reported resting nicely at the Vista Memorial Hospital in Hollywood. Though in the midst of an important production, *Sinners in Asylum*, which will launch Sarya Tarn, the new foreign import, Mr. Brand has taken a suite at the hospital to be with his little family. . . ."

Jim delivers this straight. Mr. Brand nods his head approvingly. "But, Jim," he says, "couldn't you get a little more human interest in there? Maybe about the weight of the baby and things like that. People like to read homey items. It gives Hollywood a good name, too."

"Sure I can but we'd better wait until we know exactly what happens. It might be twins. Think of the human interest you can get out of twins."

"God forbid," says Mr. Brand feelingly. "Madge, maybe you'd better check again!"

I check but there is neither a sign of a twin or even a half a twin and the nurse says it looks as though we have a long wait ahead of us.

"All right," says Mr. Brand. "We can go to work now without interruptions. Madge, telephone the desk and tell them to hold all calls and make a record of them. Put a 'Do not disturb' sign on the door. I've got a script to write."

I do all these things and we go into conference.

Three hours and several headaches later we are arguing about the relative merits of New England or the South for the American sequences. Mr. Brand holds out for New England. Social prejudices, he argues, are stronger in New England and will allow us more dramatic leeway when Tarn arrives from the jungle to meet her lover's family.

Mr. Skinner stands firm on the South. We all know, he says, how the South feels about Negroes.

"We made her Spanish," reminds the boss.

Mr. Tussler buries his head in his arms. He doesn't realize how vital a matter this is to decide, for it will determine whether Mr. Gable is to be the scion of a proud New England family or a charming renegade of the South.

It has become so heated that Mr. Skinner is minus his coat and Mr. Brand minus his pajama top exposing a manly and hairy expanse of chest from which my girlish eyes turn in proper confusion. Jim is either sleeping or making a good play at it, for he is making some very noxious sounds.

When the phone rings it comes like a bombshell.

I answer. It is Bud.

"Gee, I had a terrible time getting through to you people. I've been trying to get you for ten minutes. I finally told them the studio was on fire and here I am. I want to be the first person to congratulate the boss."

"Why," I say, "because the studio is on fire?"

"No. That's a gag. It's a boy. Congratulations!"

"What?" I inquire. "Are you crazy? Did you find the key to the bar or something?"

"Listen. I'm as sober as Brand's kid. This is on the level. It's a boy!"

I turn away from the phone a trifle dazed.

"It's Bud, Mr. Brand. He wants to congratulate you on the birth of a son!"

"What?" S. B. shoots up in his bed. "What goes on here?"

I turn back to the phone.

"How do you know, Bud," I ask.

"I've been keeping a wire open to the hospital and the kid has just been born. It's all over the studio by now!"

"Check that report!" bellows Mr. Brand.

I press down the key and as I try to get Mrs. Brand's room, Doctor X walks in rubbing his hands.

"Well, Sidney, it's a boy . . . someone to carry on the Brand name."

"What the hell!" explodes the boss. "Here I spend the day in the hospital and neglect my duties just to be near my wife and the studio has to tell me I'm a father. Jim! What am I paying you $250 a week for? I suppose just so that you can be scooped by a $15 a week office boy!"

Jim comes up out of his torpor.

Automatically he intones, "A blank was born . . ."

"It's a boy!" yells Sidney.

Love,

Maggie

7

We Can't Get Gable

December 5

The big plum of the year for a male star is again ripe for the plucking. I have just talked to Sidney Brand and it seems that Clark Gable is not available for the lead in *Sinners in Asylum* opposite Sarya Tarn. The whole colony will mourn with Sidney at this loss as everyone agrees that Gable is so perfect for the role. Our heart-felt sympathy to Sarya Tarn, too. After all, the American fans don't know her and it would have been such a help to play with Clark.

SUPER FILMS
Hollywood, California

Mr. John Blank,
Metro-Goldwyn-Mayer Studios,
Culver City, California.

Dear John:

Since our telephone conversation I have been thinking hard about the Gable situation. I had my heart set on him and although I recognize that sometimes certain things are impossible, you gave me your word of honor that I could have him. I don't like the idea of playing on our friendship, but you know that if you were on a spot and asked me to help you out I would do it like that!

I can't tell you how much I counted on Gable and I am looking forward to hearing from you that the schedules can be arranged to make him available for me.

I have in my projection room a test of a girl made in New York. She's the most exciting star possibility I've seen and to show you my heart's in the right place, you can see this test and if you like her, we can talk about sharing her contract.

Let me know at your earliest convenience about Gable.

Cordially yours,
Sidney

SUPER FILMS
INTER-OFFICE COMMUNICATION

To: *George Beck*   Subject: *Gable*
From: *Sidney Brand*   Date: *December 5*

We're being double-crossed about Gable. I want you to get on the phone right away and speak to Blank at MGM. I can't tell you how sore this has made me. Do they owe us anything so that we can make them come across with Gable? This is important, so drop everything else and report to me as soon as you get an idea on this or get word from MGM. Don't give up without a struggle.

SB

SUPER FILMS
INTER-OFFICE COMMUNICATION

To: *James Palmer*   Subject: *Gable*
From: *Madge Lawrence*   Date: *December 5*

Dear Jim:

The boss asked me to dash off a little note to you. Tell Palmer he says things are not so black as they look. That translated means that the charge is still on; the enemy stands firm; but the boss has reason to suppose the morale of the troops can be weakened by sheer bull force. To put it more simply, S. B. and MGM are tossing each other cooing little billets-doux and carelessly bandying around honeyed phrases. However, methinks I detect between the lines the glitter of steel; the sharpening of javelins. It's a toss-up who will win. Your guess is as good as anybody's. I wonder what Gable thinks, or does it matter?

Furthermore, Carsons is in our hair again and you are elected a committee of one to wrestle with the lady and persuade her to lay off Tarn. That's the third crack she's made in a week. The boss thinks it isn't cricket. Maybe a few Christian tracts will help. However, if all polite methods fail, you might turn on a little of that fabled charm of yours which I have heard rumored you use with such devastating success.

Maggie

METRO-GOLDWYN-MAYER STUDIOS
Culver City, Calif.

December 8

Mr. Sidney Brand,
Super Films,
Hollywood, Calif.

Dear Sidney:

This will acknowledge your letter of December 5th regarding Gable. If it was in my power, you'd have him but remember we have to make pictures too and Gable is scheduled to do three. If there is anyone else you'd like, let me know and I'll see if we can't wangle it.

On the basis of your friendship I ask one thing. Call off your Legal Department. I would rather do business with Al Capone.

I'll be waiting to hear from you further.

Cordially,
John Blank

SUPER FILMS
Hollywood, California

December 9

Mr. John Blank,
Metro-Goldwyn-Mayer Studios,
Culver City, Calif.

Dear John:

I am not only disappointed, I am hurt. I can't believe that you would let me down the way you have. Last night I was talking over my problem with Selma and it is her distinct recollection that you committed Gable to me. So I have a witness.

I cannot tell you how much I need Gable. It is so important that I am willing to loan you Monk Faye.

Let me hear from you.

Sincerely,
Sidney Brand

FRANCES SMITH   DECEMBER 9
SUPER FILMS
NEW YORK CITY

PROSPECTS OF GABLE STILL ALIVE STOP HOWEVER
DONT TRUST THOSE GUYS TO DO THE RIGHT THING
STOP WOULD LIKE LINE UP POSSIBLE SUBSTITUTE STOP
SUGGEST YOU TEST ALL AVAILABLE YOUNG LEADING MEN
IN NEW YORK IN SCENE FROM PLAY PREFERABLY LOVE

SCENE STOP RUSH TESTS AIRMAIL SPECIAL STOP YOU
HAVE CARTE BLANCHE STOP ADVISE IMMEDIATELY IF ANY
POSSIBILITY BECOMES REALLY EXCITING STOP REGARDS

SIDNEY

SUPER FILMS
INTER-OFFICE COMMUNICATION

To: *Jerry Freed*   Subject: *Sinners*
From: *Sidney Brand*   Date: *December 9*

I have wired New York to test all possible players as substitute for Gable. In the meantime would like a list of suggestions
from you. Cooper, Colman, Marshall, McCrea definitely not
available. Would like your list immediately. This is important!

SB

METRO-GOLDWYN-MAYER STUDIOS
Culver City, Calif.

December 11

Mr. Sidney Brand,
Super Films,
Hollywood, California.

Dear Sidney:

We have directors on our lot but we have only one Gable
and I am sorry to advise you definitely he is not available for
you at this time.

Regardless of what Selma remembers I never told you that

you could have Gable. Sure we talked about him but there's a helluva lot of difference between talking about it and promising. I'm surprised at you, Sidney.

How's the little baby?

Very truly yours,
John

SUPER FILMS
INTER-OFFICE COMMUNICATION

To: *Madge Lawrence*   Subject: *The Girls*
From: *James Palmer*   Date: *December 11*

Dear Maggie:

Took strong measures with Carsons and she went down before the onslaught like so many ninepins. From now on she and Sarya are just like that! See if you can scoff that one off, you scoffer!

Bring on your ogres and I will slay them. But when do I get my reward?

JP

SIDNEY BRAND   DECEMBER 11
SUPER FILMS
HOLLYWOOD CALIFORNIA

SENDING YOU AIRMAIL SPECIAL TESTS OF TWO MOST EXCITING POSSIBILITIES STOP I WOULD RECOMMEND

BRUCE ANDERS LEADING MAN OF SINNERS STOP CRIT-
ICS WENT MAD OVER HIS PERFORMANCE STOP THINK
CAN PERSUADE HIM LEAVE PLAY STOP STAGE SALARY
TWO HUNDRED WEEKLY STOP AM SURE CAN GET HIM
FOR THREE HUNDRED STOP OTHER MAN DAVID ABBOTT
GOOD ACTOR BUT LACKING IN ROMANTIC APPEAL STOP
ADVISE ME YOUR CHOICE AND IF YOU AGREE ON ANDERS
LET ME KNOW TERMS TO MAKE STOP REGARDS

                                                    FRANCES

December 12

Dear Sidney:

I am very worried about report in papers that Mr. Gable cannot play opposite me. It makes me very triste. I cannot sleep any more because of this worry. Mr. Gable is so charming and so exactly what I want.

Please to reassure me that everything will be all right.

My fond wishes to your so charming wife and the little one.

Sarya

MR. BRAND: REMINDER CALENDAR

December 14

Anders test in projection room at 4. Unit advised. Palmer also will be present.

Mr. Dorn has telephoned repeatedly. Says most anxious speak to you about stables. Has excellent horse for sale. (Bud says horse a winner.)

Are you dining at hospital with Mrs. Brand tonight?

Tarn ill. Her doctor advises result of worry over picture. Shall we send flowers?

Rawley has sketches which need your okay. Have arranged appointment 5 o'clock.

Tussler and Skinner advise will have sequences you want ready by tomorrow.

Barber and manicurist appointment studio 6:30 tonight.

SUPER FILMS
INTER-OFFICE COMMUNICATION

To: *James Palmer*   Subject: *Tarn*
From: *M. Lawrence*   Date: *December 14*

Dear J. P.:

Sarya heading for a crackup. We no gettee Gable. She no gettee sleep. I suggested to S. B. we send flowers. He said send Palmer. So you see how you rate. Keep up the good work and who knows?

ML

FRANCES SMITH   DECEMBER 14
SUPER FILMS
NEW YORK CITY

EVERYONE INCLUDING ME SHARES YOUR ENTHUSIASM FOR ANDERS STOP SUGGEST YOU PROCEED ALONG FOLLOWING LINES STOP THREE MONTHS GUARANTEE THREE HUNDRED WEEKLY AND YOU WORK OUT THE REST OF CONTRACT WITH REGULAR SIX MONTH OPTIONAL

PERIODS AT SMALLEST RAISES POSSIBLE STOP IF HE
SQUAWKS TELL ANDERS WHAT NICE PEOPLE WE ARE
AND HOW WE WILL TEAR UP CONTRACT IF HE BECOMES
SUCCESSFUL STOP YOU KNOW THE LINE STOP IMPER-
ATIVE HAVE HIM HERE AS SOON AS POSSIBLE AS NEED
HIM FOR WARDROBE AND MAKEUP TESTS STOP ADVISE
ME TERMS OF CONTRACT BEFORE SIGNING BUT MAKE
EVERY EFFORT GET HIM STOP IF NECESSARY YOU CAN
RAISE THE GUARANTEE FIRST PERIOD TO THREE FIFTY
STOP REGARDS

SIDNEY

SUPER FILMS
INTER-OFFICE COMMUNICATION

To: *Madge Lawrence*   Subject: *Tarn*
From: *James Palmer*   Date: *December 15*

Dear Maggie:

I have Sarya in the palm of my hand. She has developed great
faith in my powers as a publicist since I routed Carsons and
ricocheted her into the cheering ranks. Now that is done when,
oh, when are you going to let me break down some of those
girlish defenses of yours and incidentally I think you are swell
which is more than I can say for Sarya's new leading man? He
may be a good actor. I wouldn't know about such things. But I
think he is a stuffed shirt.

How's about letting me show you some of those fine old
Italian paintings of mine—any night?

JP

P. S. Sarya is sleeping good.

SUPER FILMS
INTER-OFFICE COMMUNICATION

To: *James Palmer*   Subject: *Reward*
From: *Madge Lawrence*   Date: *December 15*

Am arranging for D.S.O. medal for service under fire with Tarn. I am sure it must have been a trying ordeal to one of your polygamous tastes.

You mistake fatigue for girlish defenses. Though now that you bring them up, I shall attempt to rig up a few more to prepare me for those old Italian masters. Are you sure they are authentic? Incidentally and notwithstanding, I think Bruce Anders is elegant.

Maggie

SIDNEY BRAND   DECEMBER 16

SUPER FILMS

HOLLYWOOD CALIFORNIA

I HAVE BEEN ADVISED BY MY CLIENT BRUCE ANDERS OF TERMS OFFERED TO HIM BY YOUR NEW YORK OFFICE STOP FRANCES SMITH IS A NICE GIRL BUT SHE DOESNT TALK MY LANGUAGE STOP WHAT DO YOU MEAN THREE HUNDRED DOLLARS A WEEK STOP DO YOU EVER READ THE PAPERS STOP ANDERS IS WORTH EVERY CENT OF FIFTEEN HUNDRED A WEEK ESPECIALLY SINCE YOU NEED

HIM AS BADLY AS YOU DO STOP WE WOULD BE DELIGHTED
TO HEAR FROM YOU

HAYWORTH LORD

HAYWORTH LORD
LORD AGENCY
NEW YORK CITY

I AM UP TO YOUR TRICKS STOP YOU CANT FOOL ME
STOP BRUCE ANDERS HAS NO AGENT STOP HE IS DEAL-
ING DIRECT WITH US STOP THIS IS ONE TIME WHEN YOU
WONT BE ABLE TO HORN IN ON A GOOD THING STOP I AM
LAUGHING AT YOU STOP REGARDS

SIDNEY BRAND

FRANCES SMITH　　　　　　　　　　　DECEMBER 16
SUPER FILMS
NEW YORK CITY

HAYWORTH LORD ADVISES HE IS AGENT FOR ANDERS
STOP IS THIS TRUE STOP HE REFUSES TERMS OFFERED
AND I DONT DARE REPEAT THE PRICE HE WANTS STOP
IT WOULD MAKE YOU SICK STOP DONT LET LORD TALK
YOU INTO ANYTHING STOP I WILL DEAL WITH HIM DIRECT

STOP WHY DID IT HAVE TO BE LORD STOP ARENT THERE
ANY OTHER AGENTS IN THE BUSINESS STOP REGARDS
SIDNEY

STENOGRAPHER'S NOTEBOOK

December 16

Call Magnin's and have nightdresses, negligees, purses and other gift suggestions sent to studio on approval. Check with Mrs. Brand's salesgirl on her favorite colors.

Get catalogue various jewelers. S. B. wants exotic jewel for Selma.

Prepare list suggestions Xmas gifts for staff. Keep prices low.

Arrange purchase Xmas tree and talk to butler about digging up last year's ornaments.

Check with hospital on condition Mrs. B. and baby.

Advise house Mrs. B. returning home tomorrow.

Prepare list of guests for Xmas dinner and check list with S. B. and Selma.

Telephone Mrs. B. at hospital for list of gifts she wants purchased to complete her Xmas list.

Remind S. B. tennis lesson tomorrow morning, 9 o'clock.

Remind S. B. check on availability Harold Burns.

SUPER FILMS
INTER-OFFICE COMMUNICATION

To: *Roy Tyson*   Subject: *Tussler-Skinner*
From: *Sidney Brand*   Date: *December 17*

   Get after Tussler and Skinner and see what they have to go over with us. I've been looking for them all morning but I think they're ducking me. Maybe they're out Christmas shopping but I still want a script. Ask Madge to arrange appointment for conference as soon as you find out what bar they are in.

                                                            SB

SIDNEY BRAND   DECEMBER 17
SUPER FILMS
HOLLYWOOD CALIFORNIA

SORRY ABOUT LORD BUT IT SEEMS HE ACQUIRED ANDERS
AS CLIENT THE VERY DAY YOU WIRED ME TO CONTACT
HIM STOP THE MAN IS WORSE THAN WINCHELL STOP
HE KNOWS BEFORE YOU DO WHAT YOU WANT STOP AM
LEAVING MATTER UP TO YOU STOP HOWEVER ADVISE
YOU GET ANDERS AT ANY PRICE STOP HE IS GOING TO BE
TREMENDOUS REGARDS

                                                      FRANCES

SUPER FILMS
INTER-OFFICE COMMUNICATION

To: *Sidney Brand*
   copy: *Jerry Freed*   Subject: *Bruce Anders*
From: *George Beck*   Date: *December 18*

Have you realized that if we contract Anders, we will have two screen unknowns in the leads of *Sinners?* Is this advisable? Have just learned that Gary Cooper may be available. Do you want me to try and get him?

GB

SUPER FILMS
INTER-OFFICE COMMUNICATION

To: *George Beck*
   copy: *Jerry Freed*   Subject: *Anders*
From: *Sidney Brand*   Date: *December 18*

Cooper is not what I visualize now that I have seen Anders. He is perfect. I mean Anders. I have faith in the combination of Tarn and Anders and besides the public goes for new faces. Anyhow, the publicity we are giving Tarn is going to be enough to bring them into the theater. Besides it is Tarn we are selling and besides we ought to build up our own leading man.

SB

HAYWORTH LORD   DECEMBER 19

LORD AGENCY

NEW YORK CITY

ASKING PRICE ANDERS RIDICULOUS STOP YOU ARE A ROB-
BER STOP AM WILLING TO SPLIT DIFFERENCE STOP MY
TOP PRICE SEVEN FIFTY STOP ITS A GOOD THING YOU ARE
IN NEW YORK STOP ADVISE YOU STAY THERE IF YOU WANT
TO KEEP HEALTHY STOP ADVISE ME

                                        SIDNEY BRAND

SIDNEY BRAND   DECEMBER 19

SUPER FILMS

HOLLYWOOD CALIFORNIA

IF YOU WANT ANDERS YOU WILL HAVE TO CLOSE IMMEDI-
ATELY AS HAVE OFFERS FROM TWO OTHER STUDIOS STOP
ITS STILL FIFTEEN HUNDRED BUT IF YOU HESITATE I WILL
RAISE THE ANTE STOP DONT YOU BELIEVE ME STOP TRY
IT AND SEE STOP LOVE

                                        HAYWORTH LORD

DAILY VARIETY

December 21

Bruce Anders has been signed by Sidney Brand to play opposite Sarya Tarn in *Sinners in Asylum.* Salary is reputed to be $1500 weekly. We believe it, because Anders's agent is Hayworth Lord.

STELLA CARSONS'S COLUMN

December 21

I have it from Sarya Tarn herself, who was wearing the most beautiful beige suit at lunch the other day, that she is elated over the idea of having Bruce Anders as her leading man. Bruce is the young lad who scored so heavily in the stage production of *Sinners in Asylum* in New York. He will certainly be a welcome bachelor to the Hollywood film colony, but if my guess is right, he won't be in circulation long. The Hollywood belles are particularly fond of men of his type.

SUPER FILMS
INTER-OFFICE COMMUNICATION

To: *James Palmer*   Subject: *Bruce Anders*
From: *Madge Lawrence*   Date: *December 21*

Dear J. P.:

You had better look to your laurels because it looks by the morning paper as though you're going to lose both your girl friends. This Anders boy is already making a stir. And what is more ironic, my friend, is that you are hereby ordered to bestir yourself and see to it that the fans are aroused to a fever pitch of expectancy over S. B.'s newest "discovery." I would advise you to cease dallying and let the dust accumulate on those fine old Italian paintings.

Maggie

WESTERN UNION

SIDNEY BRAND   DECEMBER 21

SUPER FILMS

HOLLYWOOD CALIFORNIA

HEAR YOU HAVE SIGNED BRUCE ANDERS STOP MY CON-GRATULATIONS STOP LOVE

HAYWORTH

8

Holy Night! Silent Night!

December 25

Dear Aunt Agnes:

You are a dear to worry about me, but honest and truly I'm not lonely at all in my apartment and it is perfectly safe. There is a clerk on duty all night so that nobody can possibly annoy your niece even if they felt like it.

Santa has been wonderful to me this year and even though the sun shone brightly and it was good and hot, you couldn't miss the fact that it was Christmas.

Hollywood is ablaze with Christmas trees and lights, because people here are very sentimental about the holidays and all the business men banded together and had a Santa Claus float parade up and down the main boulevard every night this week featuring different picture stars playing Santa, and bells and carols and everything.

I got simply gobs of presents at the studio. Mr. and Mrs. Brand gave me a half-dozen of the most elegant nighties you could imagine, all real silk, chiffon and lace. Of course, they couldn't know that I don't like nightgowns, but they will be very handy someday if I get caught sick and have to go to a hospital.

I hope you like your present and that you had a jolly Christmas.

Happy New Year to you, Auntie, and may all the good things you deserve come your way.

Love,
Madge

December 25

Dear Liz:

Says who there isn't any Santa Claus and I'll give him the lie. For there is a Santy and although his habits are of necessity a trifle modified, due to the fact that California fireplaces are decorative but chimneyless, he gets there! I ought to know for I woke up and saw him with my own two eyes. But I am way ahead of my script.

Yesterday, the eve before Christmas, I awake to a world sunny and bright with nary a Christmasy breath about it. It is somehow sad-making but I have no time for sentimental lapses and as usual bathe, dress and breakfast in three-quarters of an hour flat and by nine A.M. am at the studio gates.

Over the gate hangs a Christmas wreath and can this be Mack, the sour-faced guardian of the portals? For overnight his menacing countenance has juggled itself into something closely akin to sweetness and charity. But this isn't the only marvel, for electricians, grips and office people hurtle across the courtyard, free spirits. Even executives are on hand early minus that nervous ghost-ridden look they usually wear. Jim Palmer says that Hollywood is a hant-ridden town; that everyone in the industry is stalked by shades of has-beens and unlifted options.

However, everyone is hantless today and only good will and cheer prevail. For when Hollywood takes time out to do anything but make motion pictures it is thorough.

I arrive in the reception room of the bungalow to find Amanda and Bud whooping with excitement over a shiny, elegant bar groaning under a magnificent array of bottled goods and glassware, all set for the afternoon's merriment.

"But wait! But wait!" Amanda shrieks deliriously. "Wait until you see what's in your office!"

Between them they propel me into my office.

I catch my breath in sheer wonder and delight. Beside my desk sprouts a tree, a tree cunningly wrought with silver, gleaming, radiant. I fall to my knees in front of it for there on a Lilliputian scale are beautifully carved figures of the Nativity. It is a gift from Rawley and the boys of the Art Department to Madge!

For the moment I recapture the same awed delight I thrilled to as a child. This is really Christmas.

The shrill ring of the phone recalls me. It is front office. A salesgirl from Bullock's and a runner from the furrier's are waiting there with a load of merchandise. We summon them and order the boxes moved in.

We are doing our Christmas shopping late. Mr. Brand with his customary disdain for time has yet to decide on presents for his wife and some other important relatives. I sign for three costly fur coats, a mink, ermine and chinchilla, and override the injunctions of the anxious runner by giving him my word of honor that we will make our selections promptly and return intact the coats we do not select. He, albeit reluctantly, accepts my signature and departs.

Bullock's boxes yield a variety of impractical chiffon and lace nightgowns, negligees and whatnots, to say nothing of handbags, perfumes, luggage and cigaret cases. By the time we unpack and hang up coats and negligees, my office looks like a fille de joie's dream.

The salesgirl is overawed by us. "Picture work," she gurgles at me, "must be so fascinating!"

"Very," I say. "You meet such interesting people."

At this point one of them breezes in. It is the maestro himself and he is wearing a pleased, fatuous smirk.

"Good morning, all," he calls. "Madge, bring in your book."

At the same time he tears off an eyeful of the saleslady, reducing her to self-conscious confusion.

Once I am in Mr. Brand's office, the Christmas spirit fades and I take down some rapid instructions. There is a note to Casting, bawling them out for sending hams instead of actors for bit roles in *Sinners*. "My productions," boasts the boss, "are always noted for their excellent casting of the minor characters and I can see no reason why I should hire hacks just because the casting department doesn't know its business. I want faces that show character and acting ability for as little money as it is necessary to spend."

Production is advised to submit breakdowns of the script and schedules for players so that S. B. won't commit himself all over the place to actors.

This, I am thinking, is really a waste of breath for invariably S. B. finds himself obligated to actors for longer periods than we need them with the result that the Legal Department has to scratch around continually for legal outs on contracts.

Legal Department is then advised confidentially that Mr. Rawley's work is not satisfactory and that S. B. will not take up his option. However, Rawley need not be notified until after the holidays. Harold Burns, the new art director, will be put on salary after the first of the year.

I feel a cold horror, for I am thinking that Rawley is one of the grandest people in the studio and certainly one of the kindest. How am I going to be able to look him in the eye when

I thank him for the tree and the exquisite Nativity? It is as though I myself were playing him this scurvy trick.

The phone rings. It is some of the bosses at MGM and they want to be sure that Sidney will toss off a few of them this mad, merry day. Sidney is most amiable but when he hangs up he says, "Can you beat that for nerve? I sweat blood to get Gable from them and now they behave as though nothing has happened. That's gratitude for you . . . pff . . ."

"Anything else?" I ask coldly.

"Oh, yes. Have you finished wrapping Mrs. Brand's presents?"

I point out that I cannot finish the wrapping until he makes up his mind about the baubles in my office.

They can wait, he says. He has to go into a huddle with Tussler and Skinner.

I come out to find my desk laden with beribboned packages and am stunned to find they are all for me! It is peculiar, I think, for I but barely know the names of some of these people who are making merry with my Christmas.

There is, too, a note from Jim Palmer warning me there will be no Christmas from him to me unless I dine with him that evening. I dispatch a note back saying I will be delighted to, but it is not because I am material-minded. I crave only the pleasure of his exotic company. I am busy dispatching S. B.'s communications when Messrs. Tussler and Skinner enter.

"Merry Christmas," whoops Skinner, scooping me around the waist and kissing me.

I inwardly rage but manage to control myself for I can see that Mr. Skinner is already on the alcoholic side.

Mr. Tussler, unaffected by Christmas, is looking as wretched as usual.

I ring S. B. and inform him the writers are here. He responds by coming into my office to personally greet the boys. He has changed his mind. This is Christmas Eve and he doesn't want to press anyone with work. Besides he has some gifts to select.

They leave, whereat Amanda, Bud, the boss and I go into a huddle to see which of the three fur coats Selma will have for Christmas. Each has its points, so we arrive at a deadlock. Bud breaks out with a bright suggestion to get one of the show girls off the set to model them for Mr. Brand.

"It's a great idea," says S. B. "Call Casting and arrange for it."

So I do and while we are waiting, I usher in a few actors who have been warming the benches all morning and are getting fretful. In between-times I tie up baubles in fancy wrappings and ribbons. Messenger boys dash in and out with packages and I realize with amazement that I have accumulated enough presents myself with which to start a modest gift shoppe.

Outside the bungalow I can already hear reverberations of merriment. Vacuous laughter and bits of song float in through the window.

"Hello, Maggie!" It is Jim. He advises me that I am to grace Publicity with my presence at their party.

Gleefully I show him all the graft I have collected and boast that I must have a lot of unknown admirers.

"Maggie," says Jim, "I hate to be the one to tear down your illusions, but in your modest way you are an important guy in this studio; you have access to the great man and can do a lot of people favors. They all want something."

That last crack echoes a faint sound of something I have heard long ago and then I remember my friend, Mr. Sellers, Max to you, who gave me my first lesson in Hollywood ways and manners and who got off to that one as a starter. I have lived a lifetime since then.

"It isn't true of everyone!" I burst out; then realize I am being unnecessarily vehement about it. For I am sure Art Department fixed the tree just to please me. I point to it in mute evidence.

"It's beautiful, Maggie," says Jim quietly. "Don't listen to me. I'm just an old sour-puss."

Then I remember about Rawley and am on the point of blubbering.

"Darling . . ." Jim starts. "I didn't mean . . ."

The phone rings. It is Casting and they are sending a model over immediately.

"Why don't you stay, Jim?" I suggested cattily. "A beautiful model is coming over to help S. B. decide on Selma's coat. If you like I'll wrap her up and give her to you for Christmas."

"To hell with models," says Jim. "Listen, Maggie . . ."

But a lot of other phones ring and S. B. buzzes and the model arrives.

She is a most regal blonde and seeing Jim at my desk apparently takes him for someone important, for she turns on a battery of eye-work that would make Dietrich look like an amateur.

"Hello," Jim says to her. "How do you do, Miss . . . Oh, I know. It's Miss America, 1935, 6, or 7?"

"Thirty-five," she says proudly.

"How would you like to be in pictures, Miss America?" Jim asks in a killing imitation of S. B.'s wolf manner.

"I'd adore it," she gasps.

"What's your telephone number?" he asks.

She smells a rat and disdainfully lifts an expressive and plucked eyebrow.

I ring S. B. and inform him the model is here.

Jim, after winking elaborately at Miss America, does a fade.

"Don't take any notice of him," I soothe her. "He's just an old newspaper man."

"Fresh, huh!" she sniffs, then confidentially to me across

the desk confides, "Honey, when they told me to report to Mr. Brand's office, you could have put me away! What's it all about?"

She is wanted, I enlighten her, to model some coats but to soften the blow I point out that you never know your luck. At least she will get a chance to meet the head man. This both pacifies and lures her.

However, S. B. isn't feeling wolfish at this moment and is most businesslike with Miss America.

She parades all three coats for us and I must say graces them with true elegance.

We are, however, still undecided and finally S. B. puts it up to Miss America.

She throws the full force of her personality in the answer.

"Why not," she elocutes, "choose the one which is most expensive?"

It is, when you come to think of it, a most rational conclusion.

"Just like a woman," laughs Mr. Brand, but you can see he is pleased for he decides on the chinchilla. I am thinking in my philosophical way that Miss America will go places and it won't be very long before she acquires a chinchilla number herself.

By noon there is a high-voltage pitch of excitement around the studio. One minute the din and buzz of studio activity; then a dramatic cessation. The clatter of typewriters ceases; the telephones are quiet; the ever-present whir of projection machines, the hum of laboratories, the clamor of sound departments are lulled. The slaves high and low burst their shackles and drop their tools. Every department, every stage is given over to high, individual revelry. I myself have received fourteen invitations.

I manage to escape and drink a toast on the set where Sarya reigns benevolently and creates good will and cheer by dishing out champagne and caviar to prop men and stars alike. I think it is very democratic of her, which proves to be the keynote of the

whole afternoon. For once we can take down our hair and frat-
ernize in the manner for which our ancestors fought and bled.

Little shots and big shots embrace each other affectionately
and everyone thinks everyone else is a great guy. Prop men,
electricians and laborers are doing nip-ups with chorus girls
and for one day the girls are ceasing to be career-minded and
are very impartial and generous with their favors. Today every
man is Pan and every girl an irresistible nymph.

A little of this goes a long way with me and besides I cannot
linger long for I must cover the publicity party and then back
to the bungalow where S. B. expects me to see that his soirée
goes off smoothly.

In Publicity, typists, phone operators and stenographers are
having their field day on the laps of lugubrious, amorous pub-
licists. Here the drinking is in deadly earnest for these scoffers
of the press are really disillusioned gentlemen and need their
whiskey neat.

Jim, glass raised in hand, is proposing a toast.

"Here's to the heels! May we all heel merrily and live to win
Academy awards!"

That is the trouble with newspapermen. They are all bitter
in their cups.

I stay long enough to assure Jim that I will have dinner with
him tonight about which point he is surprisingly insistent, and
then I dash back to the bungalow.

Through the studio streets dance the revelers, linked arm
in arm, in delightful abandon. Song is high, Christmas carols,
raucous ditties and seasonal greetings mingle discordantly on
the air.

In our bungalow, too, alcohol is the great equalizer. Bud is
sprawled in a chair intimately engaged in conversation with
a high executive. Mr. Brand is himself mixing a drink for our

janitor. Mr. Skinner has his hand on Amanda's knee. Rawley, Eric, and Tyson are there, too, together with big-wigs, more writers, glamour boys and girls, and a smattering of small fry. All of them exude unfettered cheer with the exception of poor Mr. Tussler. He alone appears unhappy. He is glaring murderously at Mr. Skinner but at the same time, I notice, is managing to put away his share of whiskey.

I meander over to the bar to see if S. B. needs me, whereat he takes advantage of the presence of company to sling an arm around me and deliver a kiss on my cheek.

"Merry Christmas!" I say meekly, but I can feel my face burning.

"She's blushing! Look boys, Madge can blush!" booms my hateful boss.

He gets a laugh.

"It's a Hollywood phenomenon!" yells Skinner.

Mr. Tussler then does a curious thing. He walks steadily over to Skinner and in a loud voice says pleasantly, "You're a louse!"

"Thanks, comrade! Merry Christmas." Skinner shoos him in the manner of a man brushing off a gnat.

Mr. Tussler, with as much dignity as he can muster, returns to his seat and his whiskey.

I gather up my courage to thank Rawley for his gift. Miserably I make my way to him and toss off some wretchedly inadequate appreciation. At the same time I toy with the idea of telling him the truth so he will be prepared. Then I realize that it is neither the time nor the place and at least he may enjoy his holidays free of anxiety.

This depresses me so I decide to do a little escaping myself and am heading for the bar when Mr. Skinner proposes a toast to the boss.

"Here's to Sidney Brand," he says. "He's a real man."

Everybody raises their glasses.

Mr. Brand beams.

"Boys . . . and girls!" He raises his hand for silence. "I am not accustomed to making speeches but I do want you boys . . . and girls . . . to know that I appreciate the cooperation and spirit which you give me and I'm looking forward to having you with me for many years to come. Let's make next year and every other year banner years for Brand and Super Films!"

"Ray! Hoo—ray!"

I look at Rawley and feel ill.

"You're a rat, Skinner!"

It is Mr. Tussler again sideswiping his enemy. I fear he is very inebriated, for after having his little say he staggers back to his bench and hugs it. Apparently no one is disturbed by this side-play but me.

The air is dense with smoke and thick with fatuous talk. I am very tired and would like nothing more than to crawl into bed and sleep for days. But I am expected to make merry.

The afternoon waxes to a furious heat. Drunks reel in and out. Glasses are shattered; drinks are spilled all over the room. Outside a few casualties are sleeping it off. But inside all is *toujours gai* and *toujours l'amour, l'amour*. Amanda is struggling in Skinner's embrace.

Mr. Tussler makes one epochal move. Up he rises and zig-zags over to Skinner, his face screwed up in the most alarming fashion. I think he is going to hit Skinner. Instead he reaches up his hand, hesitates a second, then recklessly snaps his fingers! After this herculean effort he falls flat on his face.

I am quite ready to leave when Mr. Brand advises me that he must be off. He has to stop at MGM before going home, but he is counting upon me to stay until the final curtain so that everything will be under control and the office cleared and ready for action the day after Christmas.

"But," I argue feebly, "I would like to leave now. I have a dinner engagement."

"You don't mind breaking it?"

"I do," I protest.

"Oh—I forgot to tell you," he says, "that you are having dinner at my house. Selma wants you to help fix the Christmas decorations. Besides, what do you want to eat out in a restaurant for when you can have a really homey Christmas Eve with us? I'll send the car back for you."

It may be an invite to him but I know it's a royal command. Wearily I compose a note to send to Jim for I haven't the heart to face him myself.

By the time I quit the lot only an occasional shout from a lone reveler can be heard. For the rest, all is the funereal silence of a ghost city.

I pile myself and the Christmas packages into Mr. Brand's car and am whisked out to the suburban elegance of Beverly Hills.

Selma, swathed in swansdown and velvet, languidly graces a couch in the living room and permits me to offer her my congratulations in person. It is going to be very homey, I see, just Selma, Sidney and I.

The homey meal consists of an elaborate dinner taken off trays in the living room. I am thinking I would prefer the more homey simplicity of a hamburger with Jim Palmer in a lunchwagon. But I squelch these errant thoughts and make pretty thanks for the meal.

Immediately after dinner, under the supervision of Selma, the butler and I go to work erecting an enormous tree. Sidney has already made his excuses and is out on some nefarious business of his own.

I climb precarious ladders and entwine ornaments and lights while Selma from her position below directs the operations. She is a rugged individualist and has very definite ideas of what she wants. My arms ache with weariness but Selma is still going strong. Her sense of symmetry and balance is entirely too acute for my comfort. In other words, she irks me.

Three hours later, Selma's artistic sensibilities are finally appeased and, believe it or not, I am permitted to leave. I arrive home, drop my packages helter-skelter, peel off my clothes, and am dead to the world inside of five minutes.

I plunge into a nightmare in which the events of the day are hair-raisingly jumbled. Then a heavy shape seems to envelop me and I fight my way out of sleep and sit up sharply in bed, clammy, fearful. However, all is dark and serene. My luminous watch reveals the hour as four.

I try to compose myself when I become conscious of a bulky shape pressing close to me. I am too frightened to scream. I try to convince myself that it is just part of the nightmare and manage to switch on the light.

There on the cover beside me lies Santa Claus. To be sure he is minus his usual red garb and cap but the beard is indubitably his. Long and luxurious it reaches clear to his abdomen.

A closer scrutiny, however, reveals that it is Jim Palmer. In rapid succession I feel reassurance, confusion and then rage. Violently I shake him. He doesn't respond. I am not surprised for he has brought with him the strong odor of a bar.

I climb out of bed and pull at him with all my puny strength. I manage to get a good grip and roll him over the side. Down he goes with a terrific crash. For a moment I think I have killed him, but then he emits a few unintelligible noises.

I go into the kitchen to get a pitcher of water for I mean to do this job right. There I find that the window screen has been cut, which doubtless explains how Santa arrived. I work up a really good mad.

I dash the pitcher of water over his recumbent form. He shakes, shivers and finally snaps to. "Wh . . . a . . . wha . . ."

"Wha . . . yourself," I snarl back. "What's the big idea?"

He opens a cautious eye.

"Hullo! Merry Christmas, Maggie!"

I forget I am a lady and really tell him off. This brings him to his feet.

"But darling," he breaks into my abuse, "I was lonely. I had to come. I had to be near you. . . . Besides I had some presents for you."

"That is no reason," I scold, "to break into people's houses. What would the neighbors think?"

I admit this is a weak argument.

"Look who's worrying about the neighbors," he jeers. "I'll wager you haven't seen a neighbor since you've been here."

It is true but it makes me seethe.

"Just because you are a scoffer of conventions," I yell, "is no reason to laugh at them. I know a lot of conventional people and they are very happy."

I confess I make no sense.

"But, Maggie," he cries, "I haven't done a thing. Your honor is intact."

"To hell with my honor," I say inelegantly. "It's my sleep you've ruined!"

Which leaves me as ever loitering on the vine.

Celibately,
Maggie

9

Girl Meets Boy

Sunday, January 16

I have always boasted that there are two things I would not do.

A. I would never attempt to write the great American novel.

B. I would never—but never—be emotional about an actor.

It is a cinch to avoid A. But I have gone and committed B, which only goes to show you it is flying absolutely straight into the teeth of Fate to make any flat avowals.

Last Monday morning I arise and mechanically go through the accustomed process of pulling myself together for the week's grind, little reckoning that this day is to mark an epochal turn in the career of Madge Lawrence—the Woman!

Of course, there is really nothing to prepare me for this milestone. The holidays are over. The ghosts are abroad. The slaves are again shackled. In other words the studio is back into norm.

At the office Amanda is operating on a new lipstick and Bud is examining the race charts. Since the Santa Anita track opening he has been a very conspicuous character in studio life but of little use as an office boy. Everyone hereabouts is horse-conscious and they think nothing of neglecting production and mortgaging their pay for the track. But there is nothing odd about this. It is the same with the football season and the tennis tournaments. We are very civic-minded. To me, however, it is all just another headache for it devolves upon me, besides my other duties, to be a policeman and remind our staff whenever I corner them that we are making a picture.

I notice by my memo pad that Mr. Anders is expected on the noon plane from New York today. I phone Publicity and remind them to meet our new star at the airport and give him the royal welcome. I also leave a message for Jim to be ready to report to Mr. Brand as soon as the boss arrives. I then plunge into a mass of work, hoping a vain hope to clear the decks and be ready for action, but too soon the royal dog-cart rolls up to the bungalow and ejects the great Brand.

He is in unusually fine fettle so I think perhaps he has broken his seven years of bad luck on the turf. He is hardly in the door when he yells for our racing expert to come into his office. The budding executive squares his padded shoulders and bounces in importantly. I begin to think maybe there is really a method to Bud's angles.

I phone Publicity and invite Jim to join us. He seizes the opportunity to be personal with me, but I am frigid. Since his nocturnal visit to me at Christmas I have not been very intimate with him, for although my ruinous sense of humor permitted me subsequently to laugh it off, I think it is perhaps best to discourage a gentleman whose behavior is so eccentric.

When Jim appears, Bud is still conferencing about equine matters with S. B.

"The emininent publicist," I says loftily, "will have to take a back seat until the boss has decided definitely on how to lose a few thousand dollars."

"Haven't I been punished enough?" pleads Jim. Never, he adds, in his wayward life has he crawled to a femme as he has to me.

"It is most complimentary," I say coldly, "but why step out of character for me?"

He is willing, he assures me recklessly, to do more than that to cull my favor.

"My favors," I say fractiously, "are definitely not in the market. I am fed up on being treated like a lady of joy."

"You misunderstand me," he says.

"That would be impossible," I cut in. "I have met a few gentlemen in my time and I know how to sort the lambs from the wolves and, James Palmer, despite your insidious charm, you are really a wolf."

"And, Madge Lawrence, you are a prig!"

"Huh!" I snort. "That is the usual comeback. It leaves me cold."

"And what is more," he goes on as though I hadn't interrupted, "you are definitely on the smug side."

I seethe. "If we must play truth," I say heatedly, "I can get off to a few myself. You are the type of man who . . ."

But I never get a chance to finish for Bud and the boss breeze out.

"Madge," barks S. B., "get Max on the phone and place these bets." He hands me a list.

The horse question settled for the day, S. B. condescends to attend to business. My ex-admirer and I are summoned into the office. It seems Mr. Brand has some inspired ideas on how Mr. Palmer can deliver Mr. Anders into the hearts and homes of every woman in America. Mr. Palmer is for him unusually apathetic but lends an ear.

Last night at dinner, Mr. Brand confides in us, he and Selma enjoyed a profound discussion on the peculiar cycles of audience reaction regarding screen heroes. There was, he expounds, the Valentino cycle, when women went mad about the Latin type and wore Spanish shawls, then came the fresh guy who sassed the heroine and even went so far as to bounce grapefruits in her face; then came the whimsy boys who built up the screwy tradition. We are now, says Mr. Brand imposingly, reaching the tail-end of that cycle. A new leading man must come into vogue.

So last night Selma said had Sidney noticed how Viennese waltzes were coming back into style and how women's clothes were so romantic? After all, clothes and cycles go hand in hand. All her friends, said Selma, were feeling this new rhythm of things keenly so it was bound to be significant. The time is ripe for something new. Women no longer want the sleek Latin or the fresh guy and they are getting fed up on the screwballs. What they want is the romantic gallant. That man is Bruce Anders!

Inwardly I am crowing. I am thinking Fate is putting the "last word" into the innocent mouth of Mr. Brand. I look at Jim but his eyes are guarded.

"Isn't that peculiar?" he drawls to Mr. Brand. "It is the very substance of what I discussed with a girl I used to know."

I do not miss the significance of the past tense.

"You know," goes on Jim, "it just goes to show you that it isn't really men who are polygamous. It is women. That is why there are so many dissatisfied spinsters." He grins evilly.

At this point I would like to do something undignified, like beating him over the head with the ink bottle.

"There is something in what you say," says Mr. Brand thoughtfully. "However, it is women whom we are trying to please. It is women who are responsible for paid admissions. Therefore, I want you to give Anders a terrific romantic build-up to keep him manly so the men won't think he's a pansy."

Mr. Anders, I am sure, will be very pleased to know all this about himself.

"Take some notes, Madge," commands the boss. "First I think it would be a good idea, Jim, if you get Carsons to do a spiel about how women are hungry for a new type of love. Second . . ."

The phone rings. "You answer it, Madge," says S. B.

It is Mr. Blank at Metro, so I turn it over to the boss.

Ordinarily at a time like this, Jim and I would seize the opportunity for a little private tête-à-tête. But today we avoid each other's eyes and pretend avid interest in Mr. Brand's operations. Apparently the call is unimportant. Probably Mr. Blank had nothing else to do and thinks it would be a good idea to keep up with his good friend Sidney for we hear bits of casual gossip about the races, golf and the baby. Then suddenly Sidney jerks upright in his chair and his optics distend to the popping point.

"Gable!" he ejaculates. "I can have Gable?"

This time Jim and I do look at each other.

"You're a real friend," the boss babbles hysterically. "I knew you'd come through!"

When Mr. Brand hangs up he slaps his thighs exuberantly.

"You know, there's something in prayer! And believe me, I've been praying for this to happen. You know what this means? We've got Gable! We've got to get busy! Madge, get George Beck to draw up contracts for Gable immediately, before Metro changes its mind. Jim, promise an exclusive to Carsons—but hold her off for a few days. Madge, telephone Sarya. She'll be dizzy with joy. Let Monk and the boys in on it, too. Now, we're going to have a picture!"

In a very small voice I ask him what about Bruce Anders?

"Yeah," corroborates Jim, "what about your romantic cycle?"

"Huh? What? Him? Oh God! I forgot all about Anders. What'll we do? How can we get rid of him?"

"But, Mr. Brand," I protest, "Mr. Anders will be here soon."

"Well, do something. Stop him!"

"But," I say patiently, "he is on the plane. The publicity men and cameramen are there to meet him. He will land any minute now."

Mr. Brand deflates. I see I have rubbed the bloom off his glow.

"The tragedy of it," he mourns. "Here I can have Gable and this guy Anders has to get in my hair."

I am feeling sorry for him myself but his mourning period is brief.

"Jim!" he yells. "Don't let Anders's picture get in the papers. I don't want a word about him printed. I don't want to hear from him. We've got to get rid of him. We've got to fix it so that he'll break his own contract. I know . . . we'll give him the doghouse!"

He says this like a man conferring a boon.

"Even if he is a romantic pansy," says Jim, "it is still a raw deal."

"I know. But can I help it? This business is full of heartaches. I'm sorry that Anders has to get his before he has a chance, but it's dog eat dog and I've got to show profits. And that in a nutshell is the difference between Gable and Anders. Gable is box-office. All right, Jim. Get busy. You know what to do."

"Okay." Jim shrugs and leaves.

"Get me Selma on the phone," the boss orders. "I've got to tell her the good news. This will make the day for her."

I am thinking when I return to my office that this may make

the day for Selma, but what about Bruce Anders? I am sickened. No wonder Hollywood is ghost-ridden. No one, it seems, is too little or too big for security. I begin to feel a ghost sprouting on my own shoulders. I shudder. I wonder how men like Sidney can sleep nights.

But like a good little slave, I execute my orders and console myself with the thought that maybe this is a good deed in disguise. Maybe Bruce Anders is really lucky to be out of all this mess. After all it isn't going to put him in the breadline. He is already a success in spite of Mr. Brand and the picture industry.

At this point Amanda tears in popping with excitement.

"Oh, he's gorgeous! He's stunning! He's the best-looking man I've ever seen. I'd give my soul to have a date with him!"

"If you'll let me know who you're talking about, Amanda, I'll try to arrange it for you."

"It's Bruce Anders," she sighs ecstatically.

I practically collapse but manage to ask that she usher him in. I haven't the vaguest idea of what I am going to say. I am distraught. I am nervous but I don't get a chance to think much before Mr. Anders steps in.

"How do you do," he says quietly and I find myself shaking hands with a tall, well-built young man with eager, friendly eyes.

I introduce myself and we chat easily about the plane trip and the weather quite as though we were meeting at a party and found each other in a crowd. It is some minutes before I recall myself and realize the unpleasant duty on hand. I feel something like an executioner must before the fatal moment. I know instinctively that Bruce Anders is a decent sort and doesn't rate the treatment he is to receive. I experience a crazy desire to blurt the whole thing out here and now, but manage to curb it, and instead make a stilted little speech about how sorry I am that Mr. Brand is not here to meet him and how I know he will be wanting to rest after his trip and can I help him locate a suitable hotel and after he has settled, the studio will send for him.

For the next three days it is my unpleasant duty to fabricate excuses, invent delays, and tell outrageous lies to a perfectly innocent young man who doesn't know the score and who is shuffled about the studio from one department to another in a brutal attempt to befuddle and confound him into doing something that will be in violation of his contract.

The ironic part of it all is that Mr. Anders is so very conscientious and earnest about his work that he automatically lives up to the letter of his contract and simply won't provide a loophole for legal juggling.

Mr. Beck sends S. B. a note in which he loudly protests Mr. Anders's exemplary behavior. They just can't trip the guy. Perhaps, suggests Mr. Beck, S. B. can think up some particularly effective piece of knavery which will turn the trick.

Mr. Brand can and does. "Every man," he dictates in a memo to Mr. Beck, "has his Achilles heel. With an actor it is his professional pride. If we can make a monkey out of Anders in a screen test, I'm willing to give odds that he will pay us to break his contract. No weapon is stronger than ridicule!"

I am writing this choice little communication early that afternoon, when I am holding the fort alone as S. B. has, after his Mephisophelean thrust, taken the rest of the day off for the races. I am properly incensed by this foul play and gloomily ruminate that I am keeping bad company.

"Hello, Miss Lawrence."

I look up. It is Mr. Anders holding a paper sack. Very shyly he proffers it. The afternoon is hot. He thought I might like some ice-cream. I am touched. It is the first instance that anyone has taken time out of his life to think of my stomach.

We manage, in spite of the fact that we eat off my desk amid a tangle of telephone coils and papers, to make it a festive affair.

Isn't it odd, Mr. Anders comments, that though he has made many makeup and costume tests, he has never been permitted to see himself on the screen. He would like so much to do so in order to correct any imperfections of speech and gestures. (I gulp.) It is making him nervous the way people put him off when he asks questions. But he knows he can be frank with me, for I am the only person in the studio who has been openly considerate and friendly.

I continue to nibble at the ice-cream, acutely conscious of the fact that I have been more active than most in the cabal against Mr. Anders, but there is nothing I can say. He must interpret my silence as sympathy, for he goes on to unburden himself.

"You see," he says, "this is important to me. I am not content with being a one-play success. I want seriously to make good in pictures with Super Films. Back in New York we think that Mr. Brand has created a new frontier for pictures. He is the only man with the vision and integrity to break down old taboos and forge ahead to new horizons."

I choke. It only goes to show the power of the press. I think how Jim Palmer would crow to hear all this for it proves his favorite theory that Mr. Brand is his Frankenstein and that his veins run with printer's ink.

"That is why," Mr. Anders goes on, "I was so keen to accept Mr. Brand's contract. I would have taken much less money just to have the chance to be with Super but Mr. Lord would not permit it. He said that in Hollywood your value is judged solely by your purchase price."

This is too much for me. I throw all discretion to the winds.

"Mr. Lord is absolutely correct," I say. "However, that is beside the point. I am going to tell you something, Mr. Anders.

It is most indiscreet of me and may cost me my job, but I feel you should know that you are being given the runaround. In other words they have no intention of using you in *Sinners*. They wanted Gable and when they couldn't get him they contracted you. Just before you arrived they learned they could have Gable. The reason you can't see your tests is because there are none—so far. They were made on pink film and pink film, Mr. Anders, means no film in the camera. A cute dodge, isn't it?"

Mr. Anders is bewildered.

"And moreover, Mr. Anders, when they do make an actual test they mean to brutalize your appearance and mannerisms so, by bad lighting and makeup, that you will be horrified into releasing them from your contract."

"But this is incredible!" he bursts out. "It isn't possible."

"I could have no motive in telling you this, other than to give you a chance to help yourself."

"Please believe me," he reassures me, "I think you're swell to do this. I'm not mistaking your motives but it's all so fantastic to me. What do I do now?"

"Wire Hayworth Lord everything I've told you and leave it up to him. He is one man who can put the fear of God into Brand. In the meantime go on just as you have and let no one get an idea that you're on to them."

"I don't know how to thank you . . ."

"Well, when I'm on the breadline and your name is up in lights, you can give me a handout."

"We won't wait for that to happen. You'll have dinner with me tonight."

"But," I protest, "I can never make engagements ahead. I never know when I'm free so I take my meals whenever I get them."

"That's good enough for me," says Mr. Anders grinning. "I'll have dinner with you if it has to be at midnight."

He takes my hand and I think how Amanda would envy me. I must admit it is nice.

LOS ANGELES TIMES

HAYWORTH LORD
ON RECORD-BREAKING FLIGHT

New York, January 14. Hayworth Lord, socialite-artists' manager, took off from Roosevelt Field at 6 A.M. today in an attempt to break the existing cross-country record. . . .

Mr. Lord never procrastinates. He acts in the big manner, and while he is acting he manages to do something spectacular. He is in the Blue Book which should be distinction enough in his racket, but he also flies his own plane and manages to contribute his bit to aviation.

The headlines create a stir in Hollywood circles but Mr. Anders and I are the only people who know just why Mr. Lord is flying to Hollywood. Even S. B., who is ordinarily suspicious, takes time out to root for his enemy totally unsuspecting. He forgets about the race track long enough to place bets with his pals on Lord's flight. He has a radio set up in the office so he can hear hourly reports and works up considerable steam over the affair. This pleases me enormously, though I admit a pang because I have been disloyal to my employer.

However, I am really shameless over the whole issue for I am in something of a rosy fog since my late supper with Bruce—yes, it is already Bruce and Madge. The usual crop of office irritations glances off my back like the proverbial water off a duck. I plow through my routine mechanically, enjoying the while a sharp, private excitement. I find myself remembering things Bruce said and looked—innocent enough in themselves but in the light of retrospect enormously significant. Nothing can disturb my brand-new mood or so I think until Jim Palmer breaks in on my haze.

"And how is the girl scout today?" he asks in a vinegary tone. I give him a dazzling smile for response.

"My God," he ejaculates, "so it takes an actor to put a curl in your eyes and a shine in your hair!"

"You are being obnoxious," I say, hoping to divert his thoughts but I don't know our publicist.

"Hollywood is a small place," he ruminates. "At least five people made it their business to inform me that you were seen last night supping with Bruce Anders, though why they should assume I had a tag on you I can't say. However, I will confess my masculine ego has suffered a jolt. But what really wounds me is that an actor should be the cause of it all."

He is playing for light comedy but I have an uncanny feeling that he is sounding off to cover up. I am very sad about it all—I do not know exactly why.

"Jim," I blurt out, "I'm sorry . . ."

"There is nothing to be sorry about," he says fiercely. "I am several kinds of a sap but I guess I know how to take it."

Maybe I am wrong. Maybe I'm not just another flutter in Jim's life.

"It's all right, Maggie," he grins cheerfully. "We're still friends?"

I give him my paw and experience a curious desire to reassure him. I suppose Jim is right and that every woman at heart is a polygamist.

"Now that is settled," he says briskly, "I must reprove you for being most foolhardy. Not that I give a hoot about the ethics of the case. Privately I don't blame you for putting Anders wise."

I am startled.

"Yesterday," grins Jim, "Anders is an innocent lamb amid the wolves. They are preparing to put him on the block. The knife is poised. This morning Hayworth Lord takes off on a cross-country flight to break a record—or so he says. Echo answers that a certain hot-headed young woman jeopardized her job to advise the lamb to yell for the marines. Right?"

I nod in mute tribute to his astute powers.

"It wasn't an honorable thing to do," I admit, "but I got so darned mad about it that I just disregarded the fine points."

"Pooh," says Jim. "From where I sit you behaved admirably. However, watch your step because if S. B. learns about . . ." Jim cuts across his throat with his finger eloquently.

"Zowie! He made it!"

It is young Bud whooping in. "Nine hours flat, Mr. Palmer. Boy, what a race and I'm in five bucks."

The "marines" have landed.

Mr. Brand is most jubilant too when I am summoned to his office, for he has won a lot of money.

"The laugh," says Sidney to me, "is on Hayworth. This is the first time I've made money off him."

I do not disillusion him.

Thirty minutes later a whirlwind bursts into the office.

"Hello, Sidney," it yells. "How are you? How's the baby? I broke the record. I want a drink. What the hell do you think you're trying to pull off with Anders?"

I am so bewildered I do not collect my impressions for several moments. Then I see a slim young man in evening clothes, with a very knowing but youthful face with a spot of gray at his temples.

Sidney is for once speechless.

"It's a compliment to your evil genius," grins Lord, "that I didn't take time to change my clothes in order to get here. How about that drink?"

"Mix a drink, Madge," says the boss mechanically.

"Better make it two," says Lord. "You're going to need one, Sidney."

The boss rallies and while I am mixing the drinks, manages to pass off a casual compliment or two on Lord's record-breaking flight.

"Save it," says Lord as I hand him the drink. "I haven't much time. The Mayor is giving me a reception at seven."

"What's wrong, Hayworth?" inquires the boss cautiously.

"A mere trifle," says Lord. "Probably just a misunderstanding. I hear you're putting Gable in Anders's spot in *Sinners.*"

"Now look here, Hayworth," the boss temporizes. "You know the picture business. If I can use Gable my investment is safe. If I use Anders it's a gamble. Look at it from my viewpoint for once. You agents only think of your own angles."

"My clients' angles," Lord corrects him. "I'm not quarreling about Gable. Frankly I don't blame you for using him if you can get him. But why do you have to do the dirty to Anders? The man gives up a Broadway success to come out here and you're trying to get him to break his contract. So what? The industry will think he flopped and I can't sell him. Is that kind, Sidney?"

"I'm a business man, not a humanitarian," says Sidney boldly.

"In this case," says Lord casually, "you're going to be a humanitarian and like it."

"What do you mean, Hayworth?"

"Just this," says Lord, leaning across the desk, "that you can't make *Sinners* unless Anders plays the lead!"

S. B. lets fly with an oath.

"I don't know how carefully you read Anders's contract, Sidney. Just in case your mind isn't fresh on the thing, let me recall to you Clause C, Section B: 'The artist shall submit without question, objection or complaint to all revisions, alterations and reformulations made, authorized or approved by the party of the first part in the adaptation of the property, *Sinners in Asylum*, to the screen, trusting in all instances to the superior wisdom, judgment and experience of the said party and expresses himself herein as satisfied that his full recompense shall be the salary specified in Clause B and the prestige of playing the leading role in said Sidney Brand production, which recompense is guaranteed him by the party of the first part in exchange for the sole, complete and exclusive services of the artist.' Do you get that, Brand? The 'full recompense shall be the salary *and* the prestige of playing the leading role in said production'—meaning *Sinners*."

"What," explodes the boss, "have I got a legal department for?"

"To improve your golf game, no doubt," says Lord. "Well . . . it's been pleasant seeing you, Sidney. Give my regards to Selma . . . and I'll see you at the track tomorrow."

The whirlwind whirls off and but for the mute evidence of his empty glass he might have been a dream. A bad dream, however, by the looks of Sidney, who is slumped over in his chair a trifle yellow around the gills.

Automatically I make him another drink and push it in front of him. Mechanically he lifts it and takes a long draught. He is thinking hard, I can see.

Suddenly, "Get me Blank at Metro," he yells. "At least I can tell that son of a bitch I don't want Gable!"

10

We Go on Location

St. Catharine's Hotel
Catalina Island

February 18

Dear Liz:

It is three A.M. and all is still and hushed about me. Yet I cannot sleep for a mocking moon flouts my desires and fills my foolish head with fancies. All of which means that I am choked up with romance and insomnia. So as long as sleep eludes me I will instead spin my tale for your ever-willing and (sic) sympathetic ears.

The reason I have been delinquent with my letters these past weeks is that we have been actually in production, Mr. Brand neglecting all his other obligations to concentrate on *Sinners* as it is to be our prestige picture of the year. We were supposed to go on location in the beginning, but Mr. Brand was dissatisfied with the writing of the island sequences, so instead we started at the middle of the script, working on studio stages.

Now that we are really before the cameras I think maybe I will have a breathing spell, for, I argue, there is nothing a secretary can do that will help make a film. But I am as usual dead wrong. Sidney is determined to give this everything he has, which translated means that I cease entirely to become a human being and instead am a dynamo on a twenty-four-hour shift.

I forget what it is to have a home. My days are divided between the office and the stages, for Mr. Brand feels that the company cannot afford to have him missing out on anything that is going on. So I develop a neat trick of being in two places at once for him. I am forever sprinting back and forth to the stages reminding Mr. Faye that S. B. wants a scene shot this way; that Miss Tarn must be lit so; that the company must hold everything until Mr. Brand can manage to get there and show our scenarists how to really write a scene. And when the day's grind ceases we all adjourn to the projection room where we sit until dawn watching an accumulation of rushes.

Hours of looking at the rough cut of film produces in me an optic and mental insensibility. But neither time nor tide can daunt my rapacious boss for he goes merrily on determining which of thirty-nine takes will best grace the finished film. An over-ebullient newspaperman once tagged Sidney as "Sure-Hit Brand" and to fill his column credited S. B. with a genius for the perfection of atmospheric detail which together with his astute flair for casting is intrinsically responsible for the perfect Brand film. Ever since then my boss has been busy living up to the Brand myth.

Life in a projection room is altogether *intime*, just Sidney, the cutter, the cutter's assistant and I. Being marooned for the night before a silver screen makes for a feverish camaraderie in which S. B. for one indulges with great vim. Here he can make a big display of his democracy before a small and discreet audience. He borrows cigarets and cigars indiscriminately; even going so far as to offer his own when and if he has them. In between stretches of film, he takes time out for paternalistic inquiries into our private lives, never recognizing the fact that he has deprived us of civil rights. He approaches all points with boyish zest and humor calculated to be irresistible. I learn to laugh at his quips as the simplest course. He hounds the cutters with the most impossible requests but they who have renounced home, wife and country are men of great tact and patience and never once give in to the desire to glance a blow off the Brandian proboscis, but bow and scrape and do their parts like the good little soldiers they are.

My sole pleasure in this trying nocturnal session is a purely private one for I am interested in Mr. Anders's progress and am pleased mightily with the way he acquits himself on the screen. I comment on this to the head cutter who agrees with me. We both look to S. B. for approbation but are squelched by his indifference.

"Every time I look at Anders," he mourns, "I think of how perfect Gable would have been."

Please don't think this ungenerous of Sidney for he is like an elephant who can't forget and Mr. Anders, unwittingly, has provided him with some unforgettable moments.

When dawn breaks we are still hard at it and it isn't until normal citizens are rising that Mr. Brand is satisfied we have done a "day's" work. We then lift up our weary frames from the chairs and emerge like so many zombies making their entrance into the earth world.

For Sidney this is a signal for home and bed. For us it is merely a chance to get a change of clothes, some coffee and back to the studio. I didn't get a full night's sleep until we came to Catalina. The respite here I owe to Sarya, for which bless her despite her many sins.

Our jungle sequences receiving the final sanction of the boss, we rush our location crew to Catalina. Miss Tarn and a few of the chosen bounce over luxuriously on Mr. Faye's palatial yacht. The proletariat, including grips, electricians, laborers, transportation men, assistant cameramen, assistant director, and a hundred or so Ethiopian extras, travel on the regular steamboat.

We have erected a tent city for the small fry on the Isthmus which is over on the far side of the island where our scenes will be made. Here Super Films improved upon nature by planting its own tropical foliage and making a little island off the coast of Africa, even to changing the color of the coast line by spraying the pebbled beach with specially imported sand.

I feel abused when the company departs, brooding over the unkind cut of Fate which keeps me chained to the studio when I would give my immortal soul to roast myself on the beach for a day or two. Sidney and I however are giving of our genius to some of the other pictures in operation at Super Films.

We operate this way without any unusual break or variation until one night late at the studio when Sidney and I are working. Then Catalina calls. There is nothing unusual about this as we talk to Catalina every night. I pick up my phone and listen in for I have to make notes of new schedule and possible changes.

It is Sarya's maid and she is sobbing violently in a meaningless jumble of words. I hear Sidney on his phone shouting to her to be distinct. "Oh! oh!" wails the maddening girl; then I hear a sickening thud followed by silence. Maybe Sarya has killed her. Certainly she has felled her.

S. B. jiggles the phone energetically. After a pause, operator informs us nasally that we are still connected. A new voice comes over the phone. It is Sarya's secretary. All she will say is that Sarya is ill and unhappy and nothing will content her but that Mr. Brand come to Catalina immediately.

By this time the boss is yelling murder. He insists on speaking to Sarya herself. I hear scrappy sounds of negotiation at

Catalina and then Sarya arrives at the phone. Her voice is honeyed and even and if I am any judge she is quite healthy.

"Oh, Sidney," she coos. "I am triste. . . . I am heartbroken. . . . I can no longer work in your picture."

"Is that all?" Sidney breaks in relievedly. "Now be a good girl and take a pill and go to sleep. You'll feel differently in the morning."

"I will not take a pill and do not treat me like a child," says Sarya sharply. "Conditions are intolerable for me and I will not stand by idly while that man ruins my picture. He is a drunken brute. Today he orders me off the set. I do not go back!"

"Hey, wait a minute!" yells Sidney. "Who's drunk and what's it all about?"

"Just this," hisses Sarya venomously. "Everyone is in a conspiracy to ruin me. The cameraman is deliberately spoiling my shots; Anders plays his scenes with me as though I am a load of hay; the electricians do not light me properly; the hairdresser is insolent; and Mr. Faye is drunk. Yes, drunk . . . disgustingly drunk, and ordered me off the set. . . ."

I can tell by Sidney's stunned silence that he is impressed.

"That son of a bitch!" he roars. "I'll show him if he can get drunk on my picture. He can't do this to me. I'll get another director. I'll ruin him. I'll blackball him in Hollywood. . . ."

"Oh, Sidney." Sarya is cooing again. "I knew you would understand. . . ."

"I'll be there in the morning," Sidney yells.

By courtesy of a special plane which adds several hundreds to production costs we arrive early. S. B., Roy Tyson, Jim, the writers and I. We are prepared for all contingencies, but particularly is the boss anxious that no unpleasant publicity escape from location. I, Madge, cease being studio-minded the moment I climb into the plane. I have a new bathing suit stuffed into my portable typewriter case together with a toothbrush and am prepared for a long vacation.

A studio car meets us at the landing field and we drive along the coast toward the St. Catharine's Hotel. Though the harbor is jammed with pleasure craft of every description, they do not obscure the deep, thrilling blue of the bay. To the right of us rise scraggy hills upon which are nestled picturesque little cottages which remind me of my careless New England summers and put me altogether in a holiday mood.

However, we are not on a holiday, for we have no sooner arrived at the hotel when the boss is ordering suites indiscriminately and shouting a list of instructions to me. Mr. Faye is not in his room, but Miss Tarn will be delighted if Sidney will have breakfast with her in her suite. Sidney is agreeable to the idea but first wishes to ascertain Mr. Faye's whereabouts. I phone the Isthmus and learn that Mr. Faye slept on his yacht the night before and has not yet appeared. S. B. advises me to leave word for Monk to phone him as soon as he shows up.

This allows for a delightful pause in events so that Sidney can breakfast in leisure with Sarya and the boys and I are actually on the loose for the time being. I gulp a hasty breakfast and bounce out on the sands in my new aquamarine suit, Jim having generously offered to stand by and hail me if there is an emergency call from the boss.

Picture me a gay carefree sprite tripping along the sands enjoying for the nonce the sun-kissed blessings of Catalina as made possible by the chewing-gum king to the masses of America. It is not, I decide, unlike Coney Island in feeling and spirit even if it does try to wear a rakish, Latin air, for all the officials and workers on the island are tricked out in gay Spanish effects. It is, however, a really enchanted spot completely tropical in foliage and scrubby little hills and rocks, even if

American enterprise has managed to obscure that fact with its candy and food concessions.

"Yoo—hoo, Miss Law—rence! Yoo—hoo!"

I am stopped by a petite and fair little damsel who pants up to me on the run.

"I just heard," she gasps, "Mr. Brand is here. You remember me, don't you? I'm Myrtle Standish and I'm in the picture. We've had a terrible time. Oh, my, it's been awful...."

I then have a dim recollection of an altercation over a soubrette to play a bit as a giddy chit who with Bruce and some others is shipwrecked on the island off the coast of Africa. If memory serves me Myrtle got the job because she was a friend of the head cameraman, Tom Dillon.

"Honestly, Miss Lawrence, I know I can talk to you frankly but everything is simply too haywire. I've been on location before—I've been in the business since I was five—but I tell you this is the limit. That woman is a creature..."

I have no mind to listen to gossip but a vague idea forms in the back of my mind that what Myrtle has to say might light up a murky situation.

"She's a she-wolf, Miss Lawrence, an absolute she-wolf. I've met up with a lot of he-wolves in the studios in my times," and here Myrtle rolls her china-blue eyes expressively, "but this is the first time I have known a she-wolf. The way she chases men would simply put you away! Why nothing will satisfy her but she must have them all. Why she even tried to get Tom and when he balked she behaved like a—uh—she-wolf."

So my memory serves me right. This is Tom Dillon's friend.

"He's awfully handsome, isn't he?" sighs Myrtle. "Personally, I couldn't be interested in a man unless he was handsome, though honestly some of the g-nomies these picture actresses make up to would put you away! Well, anyhow, Tom, you see got one of Tarn's invitations the other evening to visit with her in her tent. Well, we all knew what that meant because by this time even the extras are on to Tarn. So Tom got a lot of kidding from the boys and is he sore? Anyhow, everyone knew we were that way about each other so Tarn had a lot of nerve, don't you think?

"Tom gets embarrassed about it all so he tells her off in plain language. That starts her off and she accuses Tom of discriminating against her and spoiling her scenes and demands that he get fired! Can you beat it? Everyone in the business knows Tom is a great guy and one of the finest cameramen and he would never let anything personal come between him and his camera. . . .

"Well, anyway, she gets Mr. Rethberg—he's the assistant director you know, and a foreigner and they talk the same lingo. He swallows everything whole and she tells him that she wants him to direct the picture and if he will do what she says, she will get Mr. Faye off the picture and she will make a big director out of Mr. Rethberg.

"So poor Mr. Rethberg believes her and Mr. Faye has trouble with him on the set and if Mr. Rethberg thinks Tarn will back him up he's crazy! Because she backs right down and lets him take the rap, so then Mr. Rethberg gets sore and he spills the beans and Mr. Faye gets mad.

"Honestly, that man is an angel to put up with what he has . . . and yesterday she just got too much for even him when she started on Mr. Anders and said, 'The man is a clod—he has no sparkle!'"

Myrtle gets this off in such a wicked caricature of Sarya that I cannot help laughing.

Myrtle laughs too.

"I'm pretty good," she says candidly. "I'm going to be a star someday when dames like Sarya are back in Europe digging for potatoes, only I think maybe there's something wrong with my name. It doesn't work out right with numerology. Not that I am superstitious but look what happened to Carole Lombard when she stuck that extra 'e' on her name! Only I don't see how an 'e' would help Myrtle, do you?"

She might change the surname, I suggest helpfully, and then cannot resist asking what Bruce thought about it all.

"Oh him. He's all right. He never did pay her much attention and that probably made her mad, too. Maybe he's a pansy though," she adds thoughtfully, "because he never pays any attention to me either."

I do not protest Mr. Anders's normality. I merely permit myself a small elation that he hasn't turned out to be one of the wolves. I am thinking over Myrtle's revelations and trying to evolve a tactful way I can get over to Mr. Brand what the root of the trouble is. He's all burned up over Monk Faye when it is Sarya to blame. Regretfully I come to the conclusion that I am helpless as I cannot go and brutalize another girl's reputation even if she does deserve it.

I am so preoccupied with my thoughts that I am no longer watching my progress over the sand and consequently stumble and fall over someone. My victim proves to be Bruce Anders, which throws me into some confusion. He pulls me to my feet and steadies me with his hands, whereat I become conscious of the fact that the sight of him has brought on a peculiarly nervous panic. I forget all about Myrtle and merely grin foolishly at Bruce, thinking the while that I must control myself or I will betray my feelings.

"Isn't that funny?" shrills Myrtle. "We were just talking about you."

Her voice saves me.

"I hope it was something nice . . ." he says, looking into my eyes. Myrtle goes off into a high gale of laughter.

"It all depends," she finally manages, "on what you call nice."

We can't just go on and on this way so I briskly say that I must be getting back to Mr. Brand and advise Myrtle to keep in sight in the event that Mr. Brand wishes to call a meeting of the company.

Bruce offers to walk me back to the hotel, his very tone putting Myrtle off if she thought to join us.

"Everything is going to be all right now that you're here," Bruce smiles at me and he obviously isn't including Mr. Brand and the others in that remark.

To cover my silly embarrassment I hurriedly explain what caused our visit.

"It has been pretty brutal," admits Bruce, "but I imagine Mr. Brand will straighten it out. Anyway, it's no ill wind that blew you here. I'm so darned glad to see you. Could you, do you suppose, perhaps dine and dance with me tonight?"

"I'd adore to," I say with a rush which is perhaps tactically wrong, for I have read somewhere that a girl shouldn't be too eager where her emotions are involved. So just to prove that I don't give a hang about tactics, I repeat recklessly that I would adore to in the event that Mr. Brand doesn't option me for work.

We arrive at the hotel to find Jim, Skinner, Tussler, and Tyson gathered together gloomily on the veranda. Jim throws me a look when he sees me with Bruce and I know it appears as though I chased out on the sands just to find him. I blush furiously and am wild with Jim for discomforting me so.

"Where is S. B.?" I ask.

"In a terrific pet," says Jim. "Sarya got in some good work and he is convinced that Monk is deliberately ruining the picture."

"That's not true," says Bruce indignantly. "Mr. Faye has done everything a man could—under the circumstances."

"Yeah," says Skinner. "What are the circumstances? Though I'll bet I can guess. . . ."

Bruce doesn't say anything. It is obvious to me why he can't, so to cover him I quickly ask where the boss is now.

"Showing off his manly chest on the beach," says Skinner sourly. " 'Boys,' he said to us, 'you wait here while I take a little swim. I would like to be alone for a while so I can think.' "

"What about Mr. Faye?" I ask. "Has he come ashore yet?"

"We haven't heard," says Jim.

I go to my room to change my clothes and phone the Isthmus. It takes some minutes to get my call through and when I am answered, I learn that Mr. Faye is working on the set. Yes, he knows Mr. Brand has arrived, says my informant, but he says to tell Mr. Brand he can't see him.

This strikes a suspicious note. Directors, no matter how important, don't say things like that to Mr. Brand. I decide, however, to find Mr. Brand and at least relieve his mind about Mr. Faye.

I find our boss on the beach doing a good job of quiet thinking in the company of Myrtle, who is jabbering furiously at him.

"I think you are wonderful," she is saying as I come up, "and so young, too. . . ."

S. B. is beaming fatuously.

"From cameraman to producer in one reel," I gag feebly to myself and then unburden to the boss the information that Mr. Faye is already working. He will be right along, says the boss, waving me off and I know I am being dismissed.

I join the others at the hotel and we lounge around the veranda for an hour or so while the boss has a really good thinking session with Myrtle. When he finally appears he is tremendously pleased with himself and graciously suggests we all have lunch.

"Let Monk wait," he says. "Let him get good and nervous."

I have reason to doubt this psychology but keep mum. Why spoil the prospects of a good meal which is something I rarely get the chance to enjoy?

Myrtle and Bruce join us at lunch and I can see she is following up her advantage by wearing a daring little number in cherry red with a tiny bow of red ribbon in her hair.

I, for one, concentrate on the menu and ignore the table d'hôte luncheon for the à la carte menu, taking an evil delight in closing my eye to the dishes and picking at random anything that costs the most.

I am utterly shameless in my greed even when the waiter sets before me mushrooms under glass; some breast of pheasant and elegant canapés of imported caviar. This I plan to top off with hothouse strawberries. I am all ripe for the feast when I become aware of Bruce's eyes boring into me and again I am victimized by a peculiar nervousness which affects my palate and destroys my appetite. Why is it that all the big moments of my life seem inextricably bound up with the condition of my stomach?

In the midst of lunch, Sarya, followed by her maid and secretary, now essays to make an entrance. And what an entrance! She stops the dining room cold! She wafts toward us, a tender melancholy in her eyes, and extends a hand to Sidney. He goes all over caballero—rises and presses the dainty paw to his lips! I see Myrtle's eyes narrow to a slit as she takes this big. Grudgingly she permits herself to be moved over a chair so that Sarya can have the place of honor beside Sidney.

After lunch we all pile into a launch for the trek to the Isthmus. Sarya has changed into a blue and white yachting suit and crouches beside Sidney in the boat while Myrtle has to content herself crowded fanwise between Jim, Bruce and me at the other end. I am beginning to think that there will be some high comedy developments between the two girls and recklessly throw my chips on Myrtle.

Around the bay we tear at breakneck speed and pull up on the Isthmus shore. On to land we scamper to be greeted by an unholy racket. Baboons jabber a belligerent chorus at us from the palm trees; tropical birds twitter madly; tom-toms beat a sinister monotone. For a moment I am completely taken in by it all. We might be thousands of miles away from civilization. Super has certainly outdone itself.

Through the thick jungle (mostly props) we trot like a parcel of tourists and come through to a native compound teeming with glistening, dark-skinned aborigines, complete with feathered head-dresses and spears. The tom-toms beat louder.

We join a circle of natives surrounding the center of the clearing where a group of bucks and girls are swinging a sinuous rhythm, jerking their lithe bodies about, heads thrown back, eyes rolling. The tom-tom players, apparently somnolent, are sitting motionless on their haunches, their hands alone alive, flaying the drums. The effect is oddly disturbing and we whites unconsciously press close together.

Skinner, I think, starts to say something. Sidney shushes him.

Wilder and wilder beat the drums and the glistening blacks writhe tortuously.

Then over the beat of the drums comes a hoarse, frenzied voice through a megaphone.

"Come on there—give it to me! Forget who you are—you're savages now! Do you hear me? Savages!"

Then only do we see Mr. Faye as he heaves into sight crouching in front of a camera on a platform pushed by the grips.

"Monk! Monk!" yells S. B., not hesitating to speak for obviously Mr. Faye would be screaming directions only if we were shooting a silent sequence.

Monk with a blood-curdling roar leaps to his feet and sways unsteadily. Only then do we see that he is glaringly naked but for a pair of trunks. His red hair stands ludicrously upright; his face almost matching it in color.

"Cut!" he cries to the company. "Get off my set!" he bellows at us in drunken rage. "What the hell do you mean by breaking up my scene!"

"It is Mr. Brand, Monk," cries Sarya.

The sound of her voice only seems to rouse him to a greater pitch of fury.

"Throw that woman to the crocodiles," he roars.

Myrtle giggles. "Poor crocodiles!" she murmurs.

Sarya is wild.

"See!" she turns fiercely to Brand. "This is what I have been suffering! He is drunk, he is crazy!"

"He's crazy like a fox," says Myrtle. "He's shooting the swellest scene in the picture."

"She's right," says Mr. Brand. "Let him finish the scene. I'll deal with him later."

Round one for Myrtle!

We push back.

"Roll 'em!" roars Monk to the cameras. "And you drums over there, give 'em hell!"

Madder and faster beat the drums. The dancers jerk themselves into a frenzied passionate violence until they merge into one squirming mass of twisting bodies. Then with dramatic, thundering suddenness, they crumple exhaustedly. The surrounding blacks yell and stamp their applause.

"Cut!" cries Monk, breaking the spell.

"The guy ought to stay drunk all the time if he can deliver like this!" says Skinner limply.

"Not on my pictures," snarls the boss.

Mr. Faye struggles over toward us swaying drunkenly from side to side. He is certainly a fearsome sight.

He stops short of Sidney and laughs derisively.

"It's all yours, Sidney—my gift to you. The greatest scene I've ever filmed—my swan song!"

"You're drunk," raps the boss.

"You bet I'm drunk," Monk breaks in. "And I never felt better in my life and I'm going to stay drunk always and never see another camera—or—a camera. . . ." His voice breaks off incoherently, his eyes are blank.

"You're fired!" cries the boss but Mr. Faye doesn't hear him. He has passed out cold!

Two days later and we are still at Catalina. We have spent the first twenty-four hours very fearful about Mr. Faye who wouldn't respond to treatment. But now he is out of danger and is even taking nourishment.

Tonight we have just witnessed the jungle dance scene on the screen and it is terrific!

"Poor Monk," says Mr. Brand when we troop out of the hotel projection room. "It's his genius that gets in his way. He's so emotional but he always delivers."

"He is just wonderful," coos Sarya.

A strange change has taken place in Sarya these past two days. She is all sweetness and light and is doing her best to conciliate everybody, putting over the idea neatly to S. B. that if she had only realized how temperamental Mr. Faye's genius made him she would not have hindered him in any way. Now she is willing to deliver herself over completely to him. She will be just clay in his hands!

"Yeah! She's a smart dame," says Myrtle to me. We are in her room dressing for the dance at the Casino. Myrtle has kindly offered to loan me a dress.

"What has her going is not Mr. Faye's genius but the fact that Mr. Brand has been paying some attention to me. She even told him he ought to give me some more lines because I was such a clever little soubrette! Nuts! What she realizes is that Sidney isn't always going to be eating out of her hand because Sidney is a wolf and there are other dames in the world, so she thinks she had better hurry up and get herself a good picture before she speaks out of turn."

"But Myrtle," I ask with a definite want of delicacy, "won't Tom get annoyed about you and Mr. Brand?"

Myrtle giggles.

"Tom and me have an understanding, a serious understanding. We're going to be married someday. But in the meantime I want to get some place and Tom knows I'm smart enough to know where to stop. I'm not giving to Brand or anyone else. I don't play that way and besides I enjoy making it really tough for myself."

She grins winningly at me. I am thinking here is a girl after my own heart.

"I'm rooting for you," I say.

Mr. Brand is throwing a party tonight because he has finally, after Sarya apologized prettily, persuaded Monk to carry on with the picture. So all is lightness and gaiety once more and S. B. can throw himself whole-heartedly into the business of proving to Myrtle what a big guy he really is. Myrtle just twitters with appreciation but catching my eye, winks rapidly.

She wheedles S. B. out onto the floor while I dance with Bruce. Have I told you that he is a heavenly dancer? Well he is, awfully smooth and graceful. We dance every dance together for thank goodness there is no one there to cut in as Jim and some of the boys are having a poker session.

At the supper table, Myrtle makes frantic gestures to me to take a look at Sarya, who, swathed in white chiffon, is simply oozing toward little Mr. Tussler. His eyes, hypnotized, are fixed upon her in a fascinated stare.

Later when Bruce and I are strolling in the moonlight along the beach, I see the flutter of Sarya's chiffons ahead and Mr. Tussler stumbling close beside her. So, even Mr. Tussler, I think, has succumbed to Hollywood's favorite sport.

But I forget everything and everybody when Bruce stops suddenly and pulls me around to face him.

"Did I ever tell you," he inquires softly, "that you're very kissable?"

I do not answer. I just wait. His head is very close when I hear a shrill high voice.

"Well," says Myrtle, "I guess he isn't a pansy, after all."

Love,
Maggie

11

Sneak Preview

Dear Liz:

Your sage comments on what you brutally refer to as my glandular disturbances are the fatuous theorizings of a gal whose horizons have been strictly limited to newspapermen and city rooms. Why not try an insurance salesman? I hate to shatter your smug conclusions but Jim Palmer runs true to type and is already back in circulation making up for lost time. Your taunts about how I used to yearn for just such an ideal in New York leave me cold. What you overlook is the discrepancy between an exciting myth and the flesh and blood actuality. Men like Jim are irresistible between the covers of a book but in everyday life too capricious and variable for comfort.

You say my emotional hiatus over Bruce is a misdirected maternal complex complicated by my unnatural life and a spring urge. To a girl in my state of bliss that is very cold potato. In any event we are both being precipitate as Bruce has neither collapsed to his knees with an avowal nor has he yet asked for my hand. In fact he has been singularly controlled though most articulate with flowers and invitations. However, contrasting the haphazard and reckless fashion in which these Hollywood people plunge into intimacy, it is both restful and reassuring and to my mind pleasantly indicative of a more profound feeling.

You argue, moreover, that his attentions probably accrue from a debt of gratitude to me. I would ignore that crack as the scratching of a feminine claw if it came from anyone but you and would not dignify it with a rebuttal, because even in my befuddled state I can detect the difference between a look of gratitude and that other look.

You are not alone in your concern about me. My boss, too, feels deeply, though perhaps not for the same reasons. Stella Carsons broke out with a little item in her column the other day: "Is Bruce Anders hurt because our Hollywood belles have ignored him or is it true romance between him and Madge Lawrence, Sidney Brand's cute little secretary?" Don't you love that "cute"?

"Look here, Madge," says Sidney to me. "What's all this I hear about you in Carsons's column? I don't like that kind of stuff. Let Palmer take care of Anders's publicity. And besides why the hell do you have to pick on an actor? Don't you know any nice boys?"

"I'm only trying to have a little of that private life you're always inquiring about," I say sweetly.

"All right. Have it—but keep out of the papers and don't let it interfere with production."

So you see S. B. has my interests at heart, too.

Love,
Maggie

FROM A SECRETARY'S PRIVATE JOURNAL

April 27

By the time we have finished cutting and editing *Sinners*, I am so fed up on it that I do not give a hoot what happens. But in the film business it seems the fun has only just started. It is important to get an audience reaction to the film before releasing it for general consumption. That audience must be composed of paying film addicts who are neither friends nor critics and who may not know anything about how to manufacture a film but they know what they like. After all it is the man on the street who supports the industry.

Then there is another angle. The industry is very picture-conscious and if you preview a picture in Hollywood you get a strictly professional audience which is prone to be either too enthusiastic or too critical, depending entirely on personal motives. Sidney for one isn't taking a chance on having a Brand production catalogued until he is good and sure of his product. You can always improve a film after the sneak but once it is released you are licked.

For weeks we have been huddled privately against eavesdroppers to determine just where to preview *Sinners*. It wouldn't do to have anyone discover our secret, for the picture critics would like nothing better than to get a preliminary look and make some fancy predictions. Ultimately, after much cogitation, Sidney decides on previewing the film in Pomona.

The next thing I know I am on a plane with Jim bound for San Francisco. Sidney had known for a long time it would be San Francisco and not Pomona but he is taking no chance on a leak. If Sidney hadn't become a producer, I am thinking he would have made a very successful G-man.

Thus my horizons expand for now I can add a brand-new experience to my routine.

I joust with a flea.

This memorable encounter takes place in my hotel room in San Francisco while I am trying to recover from the plane ride and the brandies which Jim forced upon me to fortify me for the ordeal. However, both of us are in very fine humor because we successfully duped the boss in permitting us to come up ahead of him on the pretext that we could smooth the path for him and Selma and the others. This allows us a night to do the town.

Jim says that I have sweet blood. That is why insects make merry with me. He says he once knew a girl who was afflicted with sweet blood so excessively that a New Jersey mosquito could bite her in Maine.

"Whatever became of her?" I ask.

"She is now a very successful snake charmer," says Jim, "but strictly career-minded."

"That is very sad," I mourn with him and wham! I slap off another flea.

After a bath and a change of clothes, I meet Jim in the hotel bar and am immediately impressed with the fact that we might be in another world from Hollywood. There is here an air of well-ordered conviviality so quaintly different from our own brassy frolics. When we in Hollywood show ourselves in public we go in for startling negligee effects, our manners and speech coordinating with our casual state of dress. But here not a girl wears slacks and the only blonde in sight looks as though she was born that way. Male attire is formal in cut and if less color-ful more restful to the eye. It is with a start that I realize none of these people are in the picture business and seem quite content. That's what Hollywood does for you. It is to the denizens the only significant spot in the world and the only people who are not in pictures are the ones who are trying to get in.

Over our cocktails Jim and I amuse ourselves examining the people in the bar and figuring out their respective professions. We agree in the main but wrangle over one man whose back is toward us and whose rear view has a definitely rakish bend.

"He is a playboy," I decide after some thought.

"He is not," says Jim. "He is a broker's clerk who is trying to look like a playboy."

"You cannot," I argue, "achieve that dashing look in the rear just in off moments. It is something that comes only with constant usage. It's a natural!"

"I have given a great deal of thought to such matters," says Jim, "and I know whereof I speak. Some people study palmistry; some tell character by bumps on the scalp; some read the cards; but I have always done it with mirrors—rearview mirrors—and I know you are wrong."

I break into a giggle.

"You and your snake charmer ought to get together. Between you, you could stage a sensational act!"

"That's just like a woman," hoots Jim. "Go on, get personal."

"Why not?" I say. "There's only one way to settle this argument. Let's ask him!"

Jim throws me a look of pure admiration. I should have known better than to make that suggestion to him. However I am not one to back down. So I tuck my arm into his and say, "Lead on!"

"We can't just tap him on the shoulder," Jim whispers to me as we ease down the bar toward our quarry. "Suppose instead I take a sock at you and then he can defend you and we will all become acquainted."

"Less muscle and more brain work," I hiss.

Now we are next to the stranger-with-the-rakish-rear. Jim clears his throat ostentatiously.

"How about a drink, pardner?" he asks nasally.

Our man turns slowly.

"Palmer! You old son of a sea-horse! Where did you come from?"

Jim's face is a study. Surprise, chagrin, dismay chase themselves successively over his expressive countenance. Then I see a wary look creep in which mystifies me.

"If it isn't Stacy. Frank, meet Maggie. Maggie, this is Frank Stacy, the meanest picture critic on the West Coast."

Jim has given me my cue. I am no longer mystified. Now what, I ask myself helplessly?

"Have a drink?" Jim asks Mr. Stacy and his manner is elaborately casual.

"The drinks are on me," says Mr. Stacy. "I owe you something for that lousy deal you gave me on the Russian actress who docked here last year."

"Could I help it," says Jim, "if she had the measles and was in quarantine?"

Mr. Stacy laughs uproariously.

"So it's measles now is it? It was impetigo then."

"All right, then," says Jim. "She was inebriated, cockeyed, stinko. How the hell could I let you interview her in that condition? Why don't you guys think of *my* angle sometime?"

"There was a time back in New York," says Mr. Stacy sentimentally, "when it was *our* angle. Now you've got an angle and I've got an angle."

"To hell with angles," says Jim. "Let's get drunk."

If Jim thinks by this ruse to make his friend insensible and get rid of him, he doesn't know Mr. Stacy's capacity or his stubbornness. The more Mr. Stacy drinks, the fonder he gets of us and the fonder he gets, the more awful is the thought of parting from us.

We do not part. We all hang together through the thick and thin of one of the maddest, merriest nights I have spent. At Mr. Stacy's invitation we dine in a famous fish eatery overlooking the bay.

I have never realized before how much I like fish and have missed it until we dive into a tureen of the most divine mess of bouillabaisse and wash it down with a bottle of imported Chablis.

"They have food what is food in this man's town," remarks Jim appreciatively.

"How you can stomach that forsaken hole down south there," says Mr. Stacy, "is something I can't fathom."

"It's a good paying business," says Jim philosophically.

It's too bad we have to mention Hollywood for immediately Mr. Stacy is reminded of his profession and becomes inquisitive.

"Why are you up here? What goes on? Give me a break."

Jim, I know, has been striving manfully to avoid this issue.

"Nothing," says he meekly. "Maggie and I thought we would like a trip and a change of scenery. Maggie is very fond of fish as you can see and nothing would satisfy her but that she must come to San Francisco and have some bouillabaisse."

"You two married?" asks Stacy quickly.

"Er—no—er—"

Mr. Stacy has a certain quizzical look in his eyes, so I take advantage of it to tuck my hand cozily into Jim's.

"Jim and I," I say boldly, "are very good friends and often take trips together."

Jim gives me an agonized look but I smile brazenly at him like the hussy I am making myself out to be. I think I have succeeded in throwing Mr. Stacy off the track, for he smiles broadly back at me.

I am a trifle hazy on some points but I know that we explore Fisherman's Wharf; cover the Golden Gate bridge, which arouses Jim to emit some really choice superlatives; careen wildly up Nob Hill in a cable car and enjoy ourselves hugely, assisting to turn the car around for its descent; and wind up in Chinatown for more food and rice wine.

When we return to our hotel, dawn is tumbling in the sky. Stacy sheds a great many tears in parting from us. It is all very touching. I receive a chaste salute on the forehead and Jim is kissed on both cheeks before our friend can tear himself away.

At my door Jim lingers, apparently embarrassed for words.

"I feel a heel," he finally blurts out, "because I let Frank think . . ."

"Forget it," I reassure him. "It was in a good cause, and I think we took him in. Anyhow, it was fun."

"I don't think it was funny at all," says Jim rather grimly, I am thinking. "Anyway not when it concerns you, Maggie."

I feel all choked up. This new Jim is most unfamiliar.

"But Jim," I start to protest.

"Maggie," he interrupts, "this is probably the toughest assignment I've ever had—but I've got to tell you." He takes a deep breath. "I—I—I have more fun with you than with anyone else. You know what I mean . . . you're—well, look here, Maggie, if you ever sort of get fed up on things, just let me know."

I am a little muddled.

"Don't let it worry you," adds Jim anxiously, and shoots down the hall before I recover.

It is only after I have switched off the light and am in bed that I realize I have had a proposal!

I have a bare three hours of sleep when the shrill blast of the phone arouses me. It is my irate boss who advises me sarcastically that he is ready for work even if some people think they are on a vacation.

I splutter a sleepy apology and bounce into the shower. I am in my dressing-gown, my face loaded with cold cream, when the door flies open and a mob descends on me, Tyson, Faye and the cutters.

"Hello," they chorus. "We've ordered up breakfast."

Without a by-your-leave, they spread themselves over the bed and chairs.

With as much dignity as I can muster, I hastily retreat into the bathroom to dress.

When I reappear the breakfast table is laid. The sight of food goes illy with me and I feebly wave away the proffered eggs and ham. "A little coffee will do," I allow.

That gives rise to many raucous comments on the fashion in which I must have passed the previous evening, together with some good-natured advice on how to cure a hangover.

"Why pick my room for breakfast?" I protest crossly.

"Because," explains Mr. Faye, "Mr. Brand would like us all to hang together and your room is closest to his. We're all two floors down."

I have scarcely gulped a cup of coffee when S. B. appears.

Selma, it seems, is all broken up by the train ride and would like a masseuse to put her together again. I would like to point out to the boss that Selma is fully capable of using a phone herself but such folly is unthinkable so I sweetly sympathize about Selma's delicate health and phone the masseuse.

Sidney makes himself thoroughly at home with the eggs and ham, meanwhile treating the boys to a few reminiscences of the past when he was a penniless stripling and how he came to rise in the world. This prompts Mr. Faye to dwell on his life in the English army which terminated with the war, after which he decided to become an actor only to find himself a director.

Roy is taking all this in like so much sweet music. Doubtless he is already composing a spiel he will make to some of the boys when he becomes a big Hollywood executive.

Sidney lets fly a few compliments to the British. It is a favorite topic with him for he is an ardent Anglophile. This all reminds him how badly he felt when Edward VIII tossed over his country and crown for the woman he loved.

"You know," says Sidney feelingly, "It's hard to believe that a man could let down the Empire just for a dame."

All we need at this point is the band to burst into *Rule Britannia*.

So we spend a very educational morning dishing the Hollywood dirt; tumbling the great; exalting ourselves; and settling the affairs of Europe to make the world safe for the distribution of American films.

The air gets thick and oppressive with talk and smoke. I myself am feeling wan and limp, when about noon Selma phones to say she is ready and able and would like to do a little touring. Accordingly, the boys all push off leaving me free to tear off a much-needed nap.

It is late afternoon when I am awakened by Jim knocking on my door.

"Stacy," he hisses, "is down below. He wants us to have a farewell drink with him."

"The coast is clear," I inform him. "Our party has been out all afternoon and will probably not return until the dinner hour."

So feeling pleased with ourselves and the world, we descend to the bar where our friend awaits us with a not-so-rakish air.

"The hair of the dog," he grins, holding up an absinthe cocktail.

"That's dangerous stuff," warns Jim, "but a swell idea."

"I've never had one," I tell Jim.

"Not for little girls," says he.

"Please," I beg.

"Just one then," says Jim.

Everything goes off smoothly—much too smoothly. Jim intimates we are leaving on the night train—and offers Frank a cordial invitation to visit in Hollywood. Frank thinks we are the finest people he has ever known and he loves us both madly, when bingo! Super Films arrive en masse!

Sidney, in his usual mouse-like fashion, makes his entrance with the manager bowing and scraping before him and practically offering him the hotel. Bartenders snap to. Minions fly. The news spreads like wildfire that a great motion picture impresario is with us.

Monk calls to us.

Frank turns on a slow, mischievous smile.

"Just a little vacation, huh?" he jeers. "The hell with Frank. He's a simple-minded guy who'll swallow anything, even a yarn about a nice little girl who pretends to be bad." He shakes a reproving finger at me. "And you are a nice little girl, much too nice to be traveling in Palmer's company. He's a big bad Whoof! But just for your sake, Maggie, I won't spoil Palmer's little party because someday I'm coming down to Hollywood to prove to you that not all newspapermen are heels. I'm the exception that proves the rule! Sorry, I have to run off now, I have a deadline to make."

"Well, that's over with," I say relievedly to Jim as he leaves.

"Oh, yeah?" says Jim inelegantly. "I hope you're right."

We join Mr. Brand's party at the table. The boss is in fine

humor and even Selma unbends graciously. S. B. thrusts a small box at me. "A little present for you," he says. "Selma and I did some shopping."

I thank them profusely and can hardly wait to unwrap the package, certain it will yield some elegant trifle in jewelry.

Upon the satin lining of the box lies a silver pencil. Feebly I thank Sidney.

"It isn't just a pencil," he says triumphantly. "It's a flashlight pencil. You use it to take notes in a dark projection room or theater."

"Don't be disappointed, Maggie," whispers Jim in an aside to me. "You don't get diamonds for being efficient."

At seven-thirty we pile ourselves and the film into cars and drive some thirty miles east of San Francisco to a small out-of-the-way theater. A strong white beacon light plays over the sky as a general warning to the villagers that a new picture is being previewed. We pull up in front to find a minor mob thronging the lobby and sidewalk. There is a surge of excitement as our hired Packards stop and the autograph-hunters push forward. There are jeers of disappointment, however, as we alight.

"She's nobody," they say of Selma as she steps out.

"Hell! They aren't stars. . . ."

The mob melts magically, some to go into the theater, others to ooze on.

The cutters porter the film to the projection booth and we take our seats in a roped-off section of the orchestra. This kind of thing is a source of never-failing wonder to me—how we picture people slip so naturally into the habits of royalty.

We have arrived at the tail end of the regular feature picture which is a product of a particularly hated rival of Sidney's.

"It's lousy," Roy whispers to the boss. "How that guy gets away with it is a mystery to me."

"I hear he beats his wife," says Selma.

Sh . . . sh . . . sh . . . We are shssed.

Following the film comes a newsreel.

"I've seen it," Jim whispers to me. "Let's get a beer. There'll be plenty of time."

We slip quietly out and into the lounge. There facing us is a familiar figure.

"Hello, darlings," says Frank Stacy.

We are stopped cold.

Jim starts forward in a threatening manner.

Frank backs off. "No use trying your fists on me, you big bully you," says Stacy. "I know you can lick me but I took care of that. A couple of the boys are inside." He jerks his finger at the gentlemen's rest room.

The door opens and two gentlemen emerge and walk toward us.

"Grinnell of the *Examiner*, Stokes of the *Chronicle*," introduces Frank. "This is my good friend, Jim Palmer. And Maggie . . . she hasn't got a last name."

"Have a heart, you guys," pleads Jim. "We've come all this way to avoid newspapers. We want audience reaction, not reviews."

"You don't say," lisps Stacy in a high falsetto. "Anything Super Films does is of interest to our public and our public must be served."

"So you're going to be like that?" says Jim. "All right, go ahead. Ruin my career—lose me my job."

"Nothing," says Stacy, bowing from the hips, "would give me greater pleasure."

We watch them until they disappear into the theater.

Then Jim seizes my arm.

"Maggie, I want you to do just as I tell you to and ask no questions. First though, I've got to make a phone call."

Five minutes later Jim and I are waiting for the lights to go up in the theater announcing the interval before the preview picture. I am simply seething with excitement and suffering badly from stage-fright.

The lights flash on.

"Go on in and troop," Jim cheers me.

I fly down the aisle of the theater shrieking madly at the top of my lungs.

"He's going to kill you! Frank, he's going to kill you!"

Our ruse works. Stacy shoots up in his seat so I know where he and his friends are located. I rush headlong for them, yelling. "My brother! My brother has a gun!"

A woman screams and topples over in her seat.

Jim is close behind me.

"Let me get at him!" he shouts. "Let me get the rat!"

"Here he is," I sob wildly, "but don't hurt him."

"What did he do to you?" someone shouts.

Then I hear Mr. Brand. "Jim! Maggie! Are you crazy?"

We disregard him.

Jim has lunged forward and yanked Frank out of the row. Frank's friends plunge after them.

"Help my brother!" I cry.

"What did the guy do?"

"He ruined me!" I wail.

"The rat! Kill the dog!"

Fortunately the cops arrive at this juncture.

"Break it up! Break it up!" they yell.

Above the din I can hear the boss shout, "You're fired—the both of you!"

Monk rushes toward us. I grab him. I pretend to collapse in his arms while I hiss to him that these men are newspaper critics and Jim is trying to get them out of the theater. I suggest he go and quiet the boss with an explanation and I will escape to the ladies' room until the lights are doused.

In the mêlée I manage to get away without trouble and nervously pace the rest room until it is safe for me to emerge. When I finally come into the darkened theater and slip into my seat, I inquire of Monk what happened.

"They're all in jail," says Monk. "Jim, too?"

"Jim, too."

"You and Jim are fine actors, Maggie," compliments the boss. "All I hope is that it doesn't cost too much."

After a false start or two, *Sinners* flashes on the screen, only it is now called *Lady in a Cage.*

The fracas must have put the audience into a splendid temper for they applaud wildly. As the film unrolls, I sit, flashlight pencil poised over my notebook, for both S. B. and Monk make comments for revisions which I have to catalogue.

Accordingly, my sensibilities are not as sharp as they might be ordinarily and it is some time before the dread silence of the audience reaches my consciousness. In the dark, it is strange how acutely aware you are of emotions around you. I suddenly realize that this silence is not approbation but is like the lull before a storm. I squirm uneasily in my seat. I wonder if our party feels as I do. Nothing untoward happens until the sequence where Sarya awakens Bruce on the beach. This is a close-up of Sarya when she looks into his eyes, her "whole woman's soul aroused." She stays aroused much too long, for a laugh shatters the audience followed by a general wave of mirth.

"Give it to him, sister," some wit yells.

"Atta girl!"

Mr. Brand leans toward me. "Make a note to cut that close-up."

However the damage is done. The mob has tasted blood. During the rest of the film whenever Sarya heaves her divine form into view, loud yells of raucous appreciation greet her.

Sidney is beside himself with rage; yet he is honestly perplexed. He simply cannot fathom this ruinous reaction to our glamour girl.

In the end when Sarya is deciding to kill herself in order, so she thinks, to save her lover's life from ruin, the audience goes completely out of hand.

"Take veronal!" yells the gallery.

"Cyanide is quicker!" someone else thunders.

We do not wait for Sarya to make up her mind. We slip quietly out of our seats and in the lobby separate to take up various posts around the theater so we can gather a number of individual comments on the picture as the audience files out.

I take my stand in the ladies' room to get the "female angle."

"My, wasn't she terrible!" says a snippet in front of the mirror. "She's old enough to be my mother."

"She reminds me of Theda Bara," giggles an old woman. "You remember how she used to lie all over tiger skins."

"I like him though," I hear someone elsewhere. "He's grand. . . . I could certainly use him."

I have heard enough. I join the others in the lobby. They are all hopelessly depressed and shaken. Mr. Brand is engaged in deep conversation with the theater manager and when he joins us there is a thoughtful gleam in his eyes.

Our journey back to the hotel is accomplished in a dead silence. Sidney seems utterly withdrawn and immersed in his own thoughts.

I myself am not particularly interested in the outcome. I am worried about Jim and look for a chance to get to a telephone to find out if there is anything we can do.

We all collect in the Brand suite where S. B. orders supper. It might as well be a wake.

"What about Jim Palmer?" I ask desperately.

"Well, what about him?" asks the boss testily.

"He's in jail. We've got to get him out."

"You telephone, Madge, and find out how much his bail is."

It is, I learn, five hundred dollars for each of them.

"For five hundred dollars," says S. B., "he can stay in jail."

"It would be cheap at ten thousand," says Monk Faye quietly. "I hate to think of what would have happened if those boys had seen the picture."

"You're right, Monk," says Sidney unexpectedly. "Roy, arrange with the desk to get the money and you go after Jim."

Supper arrives and we fall to, grateful all of us, I think, to have something definite to do. We talk around and about the picture, carefully avoiding any direct reference to Miss Tarn. The photography, says the head cutter, is great. The jungle scenes are especially authentic, says the second cutter. It drags a little in the middle, contributes Selma.

"All right . . . all right," says Sidney, "but we might as well face it. Tarn is terrible!"

Now the dread fact is out everyone talks at once. I quote what I heard in the ladies' room; Selma, Monk and the cutters contribute their pieces. The consensus is pretty much the same.

"But," I say, "the girls simply adored Mr. Anders."

"You're prejudiced, Maggie," cracks the boss.

"She's right, Sidney," Selma backs me up. "Bruce is wonderful. He's got a Gable quality; only it's softer, more romantic."

"The boy gave a swell performance," says Mr. Faye. "Too bad we didn't use more of him."

"You've hit it, Monk. You're all right. I was just waiting to hear you say it. The manager said the same thing. Bruce is a find. He's great!"

Sidney gets up and paces the floor. We watch him.

"Well?" bursts out Selma. "What are you going to do? You can't let the picture go out this way?"

Sidney stops and stares at us blankly.

"What am I going to do? It's simple. All it means is the picture goes back on the stages. We rewrite the major scenes and throw all the important spots to the male lead, Anders. He's great, I tell you. It's going to be his picture. It's going to be Bruce Anders in *That Gentleman from the South*."

It is too bad Roy isn't here to say, "Boss, what a title!"

"And what about Sarya?" puts in Monk Faye slyly.

"If she gets tough, I'll take care of her. She's here on a six months' permit and if I don't want to be nice, they'll send her back where she came from."

My boss has all the answers.

The door flies open and Jim stands there grinning out of a black eye, his clothes disheveled, his collar gone, his shirt torn.

"Well, I hear I didn't miss much," he says cheerily.

"You didn't miss much? You only missed the greatest scoop of your career," says Sidney. "You missed the debut of the man who is going to be first in the hearts of American womanhood—the most sensational screen hero since Valentino—my discovery, Bruce Anders!"

12

Retakes

SUPER FILMS

INTER-OFFICE COMMUNICATION

To: *All Department Heads*
From: *Sidney Brand*

Subject: *Sinners*
Date: *April 28*

This is to advise you that *Sinners in Asylum* goes back for retakes. The new title is to be *That Gentleman from the South.* An unforeseen crisis developed at the sneak preview making these revisions imperative. These things sometimes happen.

You all know that *Sinners* has been sold to the exhibitors as our leading prestige picture and I am counting on every one of you to give me your utmost cooperation in this emergency.

Miss Lawrence will arrange a conference at which I would like you all to be present in order to acquaint you with my thoughts regarding these changes.

SB

SUPER FILMS
INTER-OFFICE COMMUNICATION

To: *Fred Cook*   Subject: *Sinners Anders*
From: *Sidney Brand*   Date: *April 28*

Line up list of all topnotch writers in Hollywood whom I can borrow temporarily to do rewrite on *Sinners*. We are making drastic story changes throwing the entire emphasis to Bruce Anders and retitling picture *That Gentleman from the South*. As we are pressed for time, I want only the very best writers who can deliver and deliver quickly.

Also have your department scour the files for follow-up vehicles for Anders. He will, I am certain, after the release of this film be one of the ranking stars of the industry and we must be prepared for follow-ups.

SB

SUPER FILMS
INTER-OFFICE COMMUNICATION

To: *James Palmer*   Subject: *Bruce Anders*
From: *Madge Lawrence*   Date: *April 28*

You are hereby ordered to spare no expense or cunning in persuading the newspaper fraternity that the only important news personality of the day is Bruce Anders. This should be a simple matter since Stanley Baldwin and the Archbishop of Canterbury tossed the late King of England into obscurity.

If anyone asks you embarrassing questions about Sarya, you

don't know who she is. Especially advise Carsons about the new state of affairs; also the New York publicity department.

There is no time to lose.

Yours,
Maggie

SUPER FILMS
INTER-OFFICE COMMUNICATION

To: *Madge Lawrence*   Subject: *Writers*
From: *Fred Cook*   Date: *May 3*

Ben Hecht contracted by Sam Goldwyn for one hundred thousand a picture. Mr. Goldwyn is taking writers seriously.

Gene Fowler wires, quote, I leave the dunghills to you. I'm looking higher than thighs these days, unquote.

Charles MacArthur is now a producer.

Frances Marion—ditto.

Bob Riskin is in London.

Kaufmann and Moss Hart somewhere on the high seas working on a musical.

Donald Ogden Stewart says why not try Benchley?

Benchley says why not try Dorothy Parker?

Parker says why not try God?

(Some fun, eh, kid? But you explain it in your own language to S. B. He wouldn't relish their particular brand of humor.)

The following I think are available and if Mr. Brand decides on any one of them I will check on salary.

Frank Mallard—he did Warner's picture on the South and they cleaned up.

Grace Riddell—she's very hot at Columbia though rumor has it she got the credit for three other guys' work.

Pat Van Ruyn—remind the boss he is a Southern gentleman himself and knows all the angles. I have proof of this from several sadder but wiser girls.

Mark Craig—whom we lost because Brand wouldn't up his salary $25. Craig now making two thousand weekly. This ought to impress Brand that Craig knows what he is doing.

Am also trying to locate Fred Switzer who is just the man to do this but his whereabouts unknown. Also checking on John King.

FC

STELLA CARSONS'S COLUMN

May 3

If Robert Taylor wasn't such a generous and really human person at heart he would be plenty worried over the threat presented in the person of Bruce Anders, for it looks as if Sidney Brand has another winner in the star of *That Gentleman from the South*. Bruce is not only the handsomest thing we've seen in years but the real news is that he can act, too, which is all the more amazing when you consider that *Gentleman from the South* is his first picture. The nearest thing to previous experience he had was playing in the original Broadway play *Sinners in Asylum*. Sarya Tarn is the lucky leading lady who is featured in Anders's first picture.

SUPER FILMS
INTER-OFFICE COMMUNICATION

To: *Sidney Brand*   Subject: *That Gentleman*

From: *Monk Faye*   Date: *May 3*

Dear Sidney:

Now that you've got everybody steamed up about the new angle on *That Gentleman from the South,* it would be reassuring to know just what you plan to do. All department heads mobbing me for instructions in lieu of appointment with you which has not transpired. Let's get down to business and have that conference and those conferences you've been writing about.

MF

THE GOSSIPEL TRUTH
Sidney Skolsky

May 4

What greatly touted foreign gal has flopped so badly that by the time her picture is revamped she will be practically atmosphere? It seems nobody has bothered to tell her about this but don't get me wrong—I love Hollywood!

SUPER FILMS
INTER-OFFICE COMMUNICATION

To: *Madge Lawrence*   Subject: *Bruce Anders*
From: *James Palmer*   Date: *May 10*

Dear Maggie:

You might advise S. B. that I am taking advantage of the highly publicized arrival of the Maharajah and Maharanee of Indore to toss a modest little soirée at the studio with Bruce Anders as host. All the hungry press, the glamour girls, and the potent tycoons of moviedom will thereby have an opportunity to lamp both Bruce and the Hindus in one take. I will personally see to it that you get at least a cavair canapé and a spot of champagne if I have to snatch these from the jaws of the Maharajah himself.

JP

SUPER FILMS
INTER-OFFICE COMMUNICATION

To: *Monk Faye*   Subject: *That Gentleman*
From: *Sidney Brand*   Date: *May 10*

Have patience, Monk. I am doing everything in my power to get things moving quickly so you can get behind the cameras, but first I must line up some writers.

Goldwyn won't let me have Hecht whom I wanted, and I am trying now to persuade Gene Fowler out of his island retreat.

SB

May 10

Dear Miss Lawrence:

Always I have thought we two were very good friends. Is it possible that you do not feel the same? For too many days now I have waited to see Mr. Brand and you are keeping me from him. I appreciate the fact that Mr. Brand is very busy but surely he will see *me*.

Sarya Tarn

SIDNEY BRAND   MAY 10

SUPER FILMS

HOLLYWOOD CALIFORNIA

YOUR PUBLICITY MAN AND YOUR SECRETARY ARE IN A CONSPIRACY TOGETHER TO RUIN ME STOP THE SITUATION IS BECOMING UNBEARABLE STOP WHY HAVE YOU CHANGED THE TITLE OF MY PICTURE STOP I MUST SEE YOU STOP LOVE

SARYA

MR. BRAND: REMINDER CALENDAR

May 10

Miss Tarn is bombarding me with calls, threats and insults. She thinks I am deliberately undermining her as you can see in the attached telegram which I wasn't supposed to read.

Party for the Maharajah and Maharanee of Indore set for Thursday. Shall I advise Mrs. B.? Is there anyone else of importance I have overlooked whom you would like to invite?

Frank Switzer definitely not available for script. Just learned he is with the Abraham Lincoln Battalion in Spain. What about Van Ruyn and Mallard? Fred Cook would like to know.

SUPER FILMS
INTER-OFFICE COMMUNICATION

To: *Fred Cook*   Subject: *Writers*
From: *Madge Lawrence*   Date: *May 10*

Mr. Brand wishes you to contract immediately Van Ruyn and Mallard. Further, if you can snag another important name or two, advise S. B. It seems the more the merrier. S. B. says to forget John King. He's been in the business too long. He's dated! You can't win for losing in Hollywood. The boss wouldn't believe Fowler was serious so he sent him an urgent wire. It may amuse you to know that Fowler wired collect that he was busy on his rock garden.

Maggie

SUPER FILMS
Hollywood, California

May 11

Dear Sarya:

I'm so sorry I haven't been able to see you but I have been very busy since I returned from San Francisco. There was so

much that piled up during my absence. I know you will understand.

I'm surprised that you will actually take these newspaper
rumors seriously. After all, you know what these newspaper
people are like—anything to fill a column.

Believe me, Sarya, you have nothing to worry about. I wish
I could say the same for Anders. He's going to cost me a lot of
money in retakes.

As for the title, *Lady in a Cage*, not only has it been used
before but the Hays office would not okay it. Anyhow what's
in a name?

Stay up at Arrowhead and enjoy yourself. You have earned
a good, long rest.

Love,
Sidney

STELLA CARSONS'S COLUMN

May 14

Bruce Anders made a charming host yesterday at the Super
Films luncheon for the Maharajah and Maharanee of Indore.
Everybody who is anybody was there and it was very gala. The
Maharanee, picturesque in her native costume, gladly posed
with the handsome Bruce and her husband. They must have
been much taken with Bruce for they announced a party at their
lovely Beverly Hills home with Bruce as the guest of honor. And
when royalty puts its stamp of approval on anyone, Hollywood
never lags far behind. It looks like a busy winter, Bruce!

May 18

Dear Madge:

I'm so disappointed about our dinner engagement last night, but it was really impossible for me to make it. I should, of course, have let you know sooner than I did and not kept you waiting at the Brown Derby, but I simply couldn't get away.

Let me have a rain check, won't you?

Cordially,
Bruce

May 18

Dear Bruce:

I fully understand about last night. It is a pretty wearying business being a Hollywood star and it is always difficult to break away from a really good party.

Anyway, as it happened I didn't have to dine alone. Mr. Palmer drifted into the Brown Derby and bought my dinner.

Cordially,
Madge Lawrence

DAILY VARIETY

May 18

Frank Mallard and Pat Van Ruyn have been loaned to Sidney Brand, of Super Films, to do the rewrite on *Sinners in Asylum* which is now *That Gentleman from the South.*

SUPER FILMS
INTER-OFFICE COMMUNICATION

To: *Sidney Brand*   Subject: *Contract*
From: *John Tussler*   Date: *May 18*

I noticed by *Variety* that you have signed Frank Mallard and
Pat Van Ruyn for the rewrite on *Sinners in Asylum.* Can I hope
this means that I may be released from my contract as I wish
to return to New York.

John Tussler

SUPER FILMS
INTER-OFFICE COMMUNICATION

To: *Madge Lawrence*   Subject: *That Gentleman*
From: *Philip Skinner*   Date: *May 18*

What goes on around here? I thought I was working on this
script but it seems I have to wait until *Variety* prints an item
to know where I stand. They can't do this to me. I'll take it up
with the Screen Scenarists.

SUPER FILMS
INTER-OFFICE COMMUNICATION

To: *Fred Cook*   Subject: *Skinner*
From: *Madge Lawrence*   Date: *May 18*

Am attaching little threat I received from Mr. Skinner. I give you the pleasure of taking care of him.

Maggie

SUPER FILMS
INTER-OFFICE COMMUNICATION

To: *Madge Lawrence*   Subject: *Skinner*
From: *Fred Cook*   Date: *May 18*

I'll be delighted to take care of Skinner but someone ought to tell him the facts of life. Doesn't he know that S. B. owns a percentage of the Screen Scenarists?

FC

SUPER FILMS
INTER-OFFICE COMMUNICATION

To: *Madge Lawrence*   Subject: *Anders*
From: *James Palmer*   Date: *May 18*

Dear Maggie:
   Skolsky would like to do a tintype of Anders, and I need your help. Anders is as difficult to find these days as Garbo. If you

can catch him between dress shirts, would you please ascertain whether he wears all of his pajamas or just part of them; and if and when he eats crackers? It was a break having dinner with you the other night. You're still my best girl.

Jim

THE GOSSIPEL TRUTH
Sidney Skolsky

May 21

Bruce Anders is famous before the release of his flicker, *That Gentleman from the South*, for he has been escorting the Countess di Frasso to parties.

SUPER FILMS
INTER-OFFICE COMMUNICATION

May 21

Dear Mr. Anders:

Publicity has asked if I can be of any aid in contacting you. They say they've tried for days to get an appointment and no luck. I am enclosing a questionnaire which if you will fill out promptly will hold for the time being.

Sincerely,
Madge Lawrence

SUPER FILMS
INTER-OFFICE COMMUNICATION

To: *Messrs. Mallard, Van Ruyn*   Subject: *That Gentleman*
From: *Sidney Brand*   Date: *May 21*

Since our talk at my house last night I have had a new angle on *That Gentleman from the South.*

As I see it Anders, the proud son of a Charleston family, impoverished by the Civil War, is a throw-back on his pioneering forefathers, and wants to forge new frontiers. His family is aghast at the idea of his becoming active in some business, but he breaks loose and takes a look at America. He finds that the men who have taken America over are debauching the fine ideals that the country stands for. Perhaps during this time he has a very disillusioning experience with a girl (I have a girl in mind, Myrtle Standish) which thoroughly disheartens him so he goes on this trading schooner to the tropics and is shipwrecked on the island. Make Anders the strong man in the island sequence; giving Tarn as little as possible. She will be the unspoiled girl he eventually brings back to the States when he goes into politics and decides it is time that honest men actively governed America.

SB

SUPER FILMS
INTER-OFFICE COMMUNICATION

To: *James Palmer*   Subject: *That Gentleman*
From: *Madge Lawrence*   Date: *May 21*

I am enclosing a copy of the new lineup that S. B. delivered to Mallard and Van Ruyn.

This is the first laugh I've enjoyed in many a day. After looking it over would it occur to you that our boss had gone almost literate? Well, the answer lies in a book review that appeared in last Sunday's *Times*, which Fred Cook clipped out for the boss to look at. Fred thought we might like to buy the book. The boss read the review and apparently absorbed it so thoroughly that it became his own idea. So, we don't have to buy the book!

Maggie

SUPER FILMS
INTER-OFFICE COMMUNICATION

To: *Madge Lawrence*   Subject: *My Freedom*
From: *John Tussler*   Date: *May 21*

Has Mr. Brand read my previous note? If not, will you call it to his attention as I would really like very much to get back to New York, and I can't see any reason for my staying here.

I would appreciate knowing as soon as possible as I have made tentative reservations to leave.

John Tussler

SUPER FILMS
INTER-OFFICE COMMUNICATION

To: *John Tussler*   Subject: *Your Freedom*
From: *Madge Lawrence*   Date: *May 21*

I am trying to get Mr. Brand to say a definite yes or no on your departure but it seems impossible to get him to commit himself. If you can hang on to your reservations, suggest you do so and I will try to get word to you in a day or so.

ML

BRUCE ANDERS

May 25

Dear Miss Lawrence:

Mr. Anders asked me to send this questionnaire to you for the publicity department. If there is any further information you would like, please telephone me and I will check with Mr. Anders.

Yours sincerely,
Mary Francis
SEC'Y TO BRUCE ANDERS

SUPER FILMS
INTER-OFFICE COMMUNICATION

To: *James Palmer*   Subject: *Anders*
From: *Madge Lawrence*   Date: *May 25*

Here is your questionnaire together with a note I received from Mr. Anders—pardon me, I mean his secretary. Mr. Anders is running the gamut very quickly, don't you think?

I know what you're thinking but please don't say it, because I'm thinking it, too. But I had it coming to me and don't you dare sympathize!

Maggie

SUPER FILMS
INTER-OFFICE COMMUNICATION

To: *Madge Lawrence*   Subject: *You*
From: *James Palmer*   Date: *May 25*

Dear Maggie:

Sympathize? Hell! I'm lousy with luck. Now maybe you'll let me buy all your dinners.

Jim

SUPER FILMS
INTER-OFFICE COMMUNICATION

To: *Fred Cook*   Subject: *That Gentleman*
From: *Sidney Brand*   Date: *June 8*

Mallard and Van Ruyn just don't get the idea. I am very dissatisfied with them. I would like a list of other available writers from you. I've got to get these retakes before the cameras immediately.

SB

SUPER FILMS
INTER-OFFICE COMMUNICATION

To: *Sidney Brand*   Subject: *That Gentleman*
From: *Fred Cook*   Date: *June 8*

There is a writer employed by Super Films who is drawing a salary and doing nothing. He is the author of a successful play for which we paid two hundred and fifty thousand dollars. You will recall it—*Sinners in Asylum,* otherwise known as *That Gentleman from the South.*

May I venture to suggest that Mr. Tussler may be of some assistance to you in your present predicament?

FC

WESTERN UNION

JOHN TUSSLER   JUNE 9

CHIEF EN ROUTE CHICAGO

I HAVE JUST READ YOUR PLAY STOP THINK IT IS GREAT
STOP ON YOUR RETURN WILL HAVE NEW CONTRACT
STOP TAKE PLANE

                                        SIDNEY BRAND

WESTERN UNION

SIDNEY BRAND   JUNE 9

SUPER FILMS

HOLLYWOOD CALIFORNIA

DONT JEST WITH ME STOP I KNOW YOU CANT READ

                                        TUSSLER

WESTERN UNION

JOHN TUSSLER   JUNE 9

CHIEF EN ROUTE CHICAGO

I AM HURT YOU LEFT WITHOUT CONSULTING ME STOP
RETURN IMMEDIATELY STOP YOUR PRESENCE ABSO-
LUTELY NECESSARY STOP REGARDS

                                        SIDNEY BRAND

WESTERN UNION

SIDNEY BRAND   JUNE 10

SUPER FILMS

HOLLYWOOD CALIFORNIA

I AM SORRY I HURT YOU STOP IT SEEMS ALL THINGS ARE
POSSIBLE STOP EVEN THAT STOP I WILL NOT COME BACK
STOP I WILL NOT COME BACK STOP I WILL NEVER COME
BACK STOP AFFECTIONATELY

                                        JOHN TUSSLER

 # WESTERN UNION

JOHN TUSSLER   JUNE 10

CHIEF EN ROUTE CHICAGO

YOURE MISSING THE OPPORTUNITY OF A LIFETIME STOP
I WILL GIVE YOU SOLE SCREEN CREDIT STOP NO MAN
COULD ASK FOR MORE STOP TAKE PLANE AT KANSAS
CITY STOP EXPECT YOU

                                        SIDNEY BRAND

WESTERN UNION

SIDNEY BRAND   JUNE 11

SUPER FILMS

HOLLYWOOD CALIFORNIA

I AM THE HAPPIEST MAN IN THE WORLD STOP I HAVE A
COMFORTABLE UPPER BERTH STOP THERE IS A LOVELY
LADY IN THE LOWER BERTH STOP SHE HATES PICTURES
STOP AND YOU OFFER ME A SOLE SCREEN CREDIT

                                              TUSSLER

 WESTERN UNION

JOHN TUSSLER   JUNE 11

ON BOARD THE CHIEF

I GIVE YOU ONE MORE CHANCE STOP EITHER YOU
RETURN IMMEDIATELY OR I BLACKBALL YOU IN HOLLY-
WOOD STOP WHICH MEANS YOULL NEVER BE ABLE TO
HAVE ANOTHER JOB HERE STOP WHAT DO YOU THINK
QUESTION MARK

                                        SIDNEY BRAND

SIDNEY BRAND   JUNE 12

SUPER FILMS

HOLLYWOOD CALIFORNIA

WHAT DO I THINK STOP WHO TOLD YOU I COULD THINK
STOP YOU NEVER THOUGHT OF THAT YOURSELF STOP
BUT IF YOU MUST KNOW WHAT I THINK I WILL BE GLAD
TO TELL YOU AND IT WONT COST YOU A CENT STOP BOO
EXCLAMATION POINT I THINK YOURE A NASTY MAN

                                                      TUSSLER

DAILY VARIETY

June 18

Dudley Nichols, Joel Sayre and Lillian Hellman are over at
Super scripting the rewrite on *Sinners in Asylum,* now known
as *That Gentleman from the South.* Overtures are being made to
William Faulkner and Erskine Caldwell for their particular
services in rendering the Southern scene authentic.

13

Premiere

Dear Liz:

So you don't think those pictures do me justice? Well, I defy even Greta Garbo, under the circumstances, to look beautiful and dignified; and admittedly I'm no Garbo. Besides I'm too freckled by now to be a good photographic subject. Nevertheless, it is, you must admit, a feat to make the front pages, especially when you consider the fact that I am not the victim of a *crime passionel* even though by the looks of Jim you'd think murder, at least, was imminent. Of course, if it hadn't been for that candid camera fiend who took the picture, Jim and I would still be muddling around in obscurity, albeit quite contentedly. It's little accidents like this that make history.

It all dates back to when I am still a cog pushing the wheels of the industry around with no pretensions to fame. We are busy on the revamped version of *Sinners* and failing to entice Mr. Tussler back into the field, the boss hires a flock of fancy writing names at fancier salaries and we really go to work in earnest tossing out the *Lady in a Cage* to make room for *That Gentleman from the South.* Of course, this necessitates giving

Bruce the glamour buildup in private life besides throwing the picture to him. Ay, and there's the rub.

My big moment, who self-admittedly is career-minded, swallows his publicity whole and goes actor on me. I admit, my sage one, that I have my bad moments. I'll even go farther than that and confess that I give myself over entirely to the business of indulging in a personal hell. I feel keenly the heavy burden of womanhood and am reduced to a pulp at the sound of a sentimental ditty. I read Dorothy Parker for consolation and feel like a woman of destiny. In my maudlinity, I live in the shades of unrequited love and I can already visualize myself in dramatic black clothes which enhance the tragic quality of my haunted face. All in all I thoroughly enjoy myself.

Then some wag publishes a little item to this effect: "What actor's surprise success has gone to his head causing him to drop what prominent producer's secretary like a hot potato? Incidentally, if rumors mean anything, she was instrumental in helping him get there."

It is one thing, I discover, to luxuriate in private over a thwarted love and another to have it broadcast to the public. Everyone in the studio, according to their individual bent, either treats me to a nauseous solicitude or comes over to me with some very snide cracks. Prominently among the latter is this blonde, Maxine Stoddard, who is very annoyed because I have the job she wants. She openly crows at my defeat.

Our office boy consoles me with his own peculiar philosophy. He says outright that I am much too good for an actor and I ought to be relieved it has turned out this way. Amanda decides that glamour is maybe all right for a date but a plumber's assistant lasts forever. Only Jim flatly refuses to regard me as an object of pity or mirth.

Perhaps it is well for me that my private life becomes public, for then I have to face the issue squarely. I give some earnest cogitation to this male-female problem and arrive at the conclusion that I am not the type for protracted tragedy. The role just won't fit. Some people might accuse me of being emotionally shallow and lacking in the profounder feelings, but I have a peculiar intuition that most gals who cry their havoc to the skies are merely enjoying the spotlight. What do you think?

Despite my amorous vicissitudes, production goes on. We rush the revised edition of our picture before the camera. Fortunately for S. B., our director, Monk Faye, has cannily foreseen some such contingency and filmed a flock of close-ups of Bruce about which the boss knew nothing. So it is a simple matter in some major scenes to substitute a close-up of Bruce for a close-up of Sarya, and while Sarya is mouthing a few lines, we merely hear her voice, while we are really engrossed in looking at Bruce. That, my dear, is how stars are made.

For the rest, our new writers, unhampered by Mr. Skinner's ideas of an Academy winner, turn out a really literate job. So cunningly is the script evolved that we do not need Sarya for retakes and much to S. B.'s relief, she can luxuriate in splendid grandeur at Arrowhead happy in the thought that her brilliant future is being coddled by Sidney.

The world premiere is set for the Cathay Circle. This means we think our picture is good enough for road-show prices. The masses will have to stew impatiently for a look at it until we have exhausted the pockets of the privileged classes.

Although the handling of a premiere belongs to the Publicity Department, all hands are on deck to make it the biggest, the gaudiest, the most colossal affair ever. This involves a high-pressure campaign calculated to whet the appetites of the paying public into a screaming frenzy to witness the spectacle. The catch in this is that it is practically impossible for the layman to purchase a ducat to the premiere as the motion picture fraternity has the monopoly for the night.

However, the bosses of the picture industry are not without charity, for we erect a temporary row of grandstands, built to accommodate hundreds of sightseers. Thus for the modest sum of fifty cents you may witness the parade of the Hollywood great and near-great as they troop into the theater. Of course you don't get to see the picture but what do you expect for four bits? The whole pageant is really an excuse to let the film people indulge in their favorite pastime of dressing up and showing off.

On account of this is a Sidney Brand production, we are assured of a wholesale turnout because Sidney is a big man in the industry and it pays to indulge him and then, on the other hand, there is a chance he may be slipping and you might get in the first snicker.

Paring down the royal list to see who will and must be invited to Sidney's own levee following the premiere, is also something of a chore. This festivity, which is to take place in a private room of the Trocadero, is sort of like a wedding where only picked members of the family attend. Jim and I, alone out of the office staff, are included in this exclusive list, but we do not fool ourselves that it is because we rate, but simply because it is part of our jobs—Jim to referee the post mortem publicity value; me to be on hand in case the boss needs me.

However, I am never one to quarrel with motives for I am frankly pleased at the chance of a binge myself. Eric, the designer, and I go into a huddle about the clothes problem and he chooses for me from Wardrobe a luscious gown in striped slipper satin together with a modest little finger-tip cape of mink, so I will do the studio proud.

I will have to confess at this point a most gratifying sensation that when I next encounter Mr. Anders, I will be dressed to the teeth. I know this is small of me and utterly female but it is very consoling for there is nothing like the glitter of glad rags when a girl has been jilted.

The eve of the big day I find myself alone at the office to attend to last-minute detail. Selma is giving a dinner party and for this once Sidney attends on time. Bud and Amanda, who have snagged a pair of tickets, rush home early in order to groom themselves for what Amanda terms a "formal" affair.

I have a tray sent up from the commissary and bathe and dress in S. B.'s private bathroom. Eric has been foresighted enough to include lace panties, satin sandals and even a pair of gossamer hose. I feel a little like Cinderella for all my trappings have the enchantment of unfamiliarity. With one last satisfied glance into the mirror I trip out into my office and there find a florist's box. Nestling in the tissue is one orchid of speckled yellow on velvety brown.

All my life I have wanted to be a girl who gets orchids so you can imagine my feelings. The card in the box reads:

"It reminds me of you, especially the freckles, Jim."

I wave my magic wand and presto, there is a Packard limousine awaiting me at the office door. This, too, belongs to the studio but is mine for the night. If I think I am going to make the grand entrance in all my finery, I am very much mistaken. The chauffeur is stalled at Wilshire Boulevard and McCarthy Drive by a host of cars, sirens, and pressing mobs making further passage impossible. I decide that it will be simpler if I take to my feet.

I alight to face a ferocious jungle cannibal, holding aloft a spear, his painted face thrust forward threateningly. I start back nervously; then realize that this is merely a living model, posed in a shell lighted from within. As I traverse the drive I pass a line of such shells, all encasing living models who represent characters from Charleston to the coast of Africa and back again.

My progress becomes increasingly difficult as I approach the theater, the mobs surging thickly in and around, cutting up a frightful din and hubbub, despite the frantic police guards. Glaring arc lights flood the circle and from the tower of the Moorish cinema temple a revolving beam plays ceaselessly on the heavens.

Several costumed flunkeys are unrolling a rose-colored carpet covering the theater walk and about a block of the sidewalk. Banked on either side of the theater walk are great baskets of flowers.

As I make the carpet, I cause a minor flurry.

"Who is she?"

"Aw, she's nobody."

"She's pretty, though," I hear one charitable soul allow.

I am seized with a nervous panic. The carpet stretches on interminably, it seems. Boom! A flashlight bursts in my face. But it isn't for me. It is for royalty walking abreast of me. As I travel on, flashlights exploding to the right, flashlights exploding to the left, my composure is utterly shattered.

Then I spy a familiar face near the box-office and in my relief quicken my steps. It is Jim standing guard over the hullabaloo, looking extremely distinguished in his dinner jacket. As his face breaks into a welcoming grin, I feel as though I have come home. He reaches for my hand and draws me beside him whispering, "You're a sight for sore eyes, Maggie."

I feel a stinging sensation on my eyelids as though I am going to cry. Women are such nitwits. We choose the most irrational moments to wax emotional. Me, I'm no different from the rest.

A roar of applause breaks forth. A long expensive automobile has just disgorged Hollywood's most publicized happily married couple.

Flash! And then I see Myrtle all done up in chiffon and white fox furs preening very happily before a flock of cameras. Beside her stands Tom Dillon grinning self-consciously.

"Hi!" she yells. "Isn't it all too wonderful? You look grand. Where did you get the duds? Isn't Tom a scream in tails? Whoo! what's that?"

It is another wild outburst caused by the advent of Sarya. She is with three male escorts and between them shows off to her tropical best in silver lamé with sable bands.

"Hello, everybody," she coos over the microphone. "It is all so wonderful but then I think everything in America is wonderful. . . ."

Myrtle clucks sympathetically.

"It's too bad she won't be here long. Europe won't look good after this. Well, see you in the movies, Madge. 'Bye, Jim."

By now there is a stream of long, glistening cars, all spewing their quota of highly perfumed stars and stiff-bosomed escorts. Loud and furious waxes the tumult. A swanky, low job in baby-blue paint rolls up. Out steps Bud, in a tuxedo of eccentric cut, assisting Amanda to the sidewalk. Up the aisle they swagger. I begin to think that perhaps all this uproar is justified if only to provide this proud, blissful moment for Bud and Amanda. When they greet me, Bud whispers in an aside that a guy who didn't pay up on a racing debt let him have the swell chariot.

Randolph Scott, Carole Lombard, Adolph Zukor, Virginia Bruce, Mary Brian, Jean Arthur . . . actors, producers, directors by the gross pour down the aisle to the ever deafening chorus of cheers and yells. Then my boss elects to appear, Selma in her chinchilla wrap, and a party of people with them.

Jim steps out of line to do his duty and cajoles S. B. over to the mike.

"Hello, folks," Sidney greets them coyly. "I wish you were all here so that we could together be thrilled by what I know is a magnificent picture. However, it isn't me you want to hear from so I'll introduce Bruce Anders, star of *That Gentleman from the South*, who is the real hero of this occasion."

It is only then that I notice Bruce lurking beside Sidney. The blonde clinging to his arm and looking tenderly at him is, dear, no other than my friend, the fishwife, whom I met at my debut in the Cocoanut Grove! Hollywood is a small place.

I know you are wanting to get a load of how I think and feel at this point. Well, did you ever have a bad dream and wake up to laugh at your foolish fancies? That's about the sum and total of it for Mr. Anders looks vaguely like someone I once knew. The familiarity is, however, fleeting.

Only Jim, as he steps back beside me, is real . . . and now everything is beautifully, blindingly clear to me. I want to blurt out to him, "Look here, a very queer thing has just happened. It's really quite wonderful. I adore the way your hair stands up on end, the way your eyes crinkle when you smile. I even like that jackdaw strut of yours. In fact, I like every foolish thing about you. In other words, toots, I love you."

And he would say, "Madame, you have absolutely no sense of the fitness of things. What do you expect me to do about it now?"

"That's what is so swell about it," I would respond. "You don't have to do a single blessed thing except hold my hand and look at me the way you do and make me realize that you are here and I'm beside you and all is very right with the world."

Flash! I am roused out of my reverie. The crowds are applauding Bruce as he leaves the microphone. He is bowing gracefully. S. B. motions us to join them. He wants Jim and me to go ahead to the Trocadero after the premiere to see that everything is in order.

"Hello, Palmer. Hello, Madge," says Bruce. "This is all very exciting, isn't it?"

I wish him every success.

"You know, you should really have been up at the mike with me." He laughs nervously. "Come to think of it, I really owe this all to you, Madge."

"What do you mean you owe it to her?" says my snoopy boss.

Jim interrupts quickly, "It's time to go in, S. B."

Inside the theater the second act of the comedy is in full swing. The befurred and bejeweled ladies are still strutting self-consciously for Hymie Fink is doubtless lurking somewhere. Mr. Fink is a curious figure in the film capital. He pops up at all functions to take candid camera shots. It wouldn't do to let down a minute while he is around. In fact, we don't let down until the lights are doused.

That Gentleman from the South is now cinema history so let it suffice that the applause is more spirited than ever, that a new star skyrockets in the Hollywood heavens, and that once more Sidney Brand proves incontrovertibly that his touch is infallible.

When the last finis is written upon the screen, Sidney and Bruce are mobbed by well-wishers while Jim and I round up the studio Packard.

"Did I tell you," remarks Jim as he helps me into the car, "that you are probably the most ravishing creature I've ever seen?"

"Thanks," I say, "but it is Eric who rates the compliment."

"No, Maggie," he disagrees. "There's an extra special shiny look about you tonight."

"All the better to dazzle you with," I mumble a bit shakily.

"Maggie!"

Jim's hand tightens like a vise on my arm.

I look squarely up at him. My face must be a dead give-away for immediately I am engulfed in the most undignified but entirely satisfying embrace.

It is some minutes before I gain my breath to tell Jim of how it all happened to me and want to know how he knew about himself. He confesses it was Christmas night when he blundered like such an idiot and was very tight but wanted desperately to let me know how he felt, and I thought he was clowning and what hell it was for him when he thought I cared for Bruce, and how we will have a house in the hills and I will learn to cook and everything will be swell.

By then we are at the Trocadero and it is two very disheveled people who alight from the car. We don't give a damn what people think and walk in hand in hand like the babes in the wood.

Mr. Brand's party is in a room off the bar. We do not have any time for ourselves for the hungry guests are already beginning to pile in, and in lieu of the hosts, we greet them and make them feel at home, at the same time interchanging unashamedly glad little looks with each other and isn't it curious how at a sacred time like this your tummy feels most affected for mine is lurching about crazily as though it were a separate entity.

There are no trumpets to announce the arrival of the really important people, but Hymie Fink heaves into sight so they can't be far behind, which proves to be true for Sidney, Selma, Bruce, the Blonde and their entourage make their triumphant entrance.

Jim seizes this opportunity to grab me by the hand and duck out from the mob and upstairs to where the music is playing. It is with a shock that I realize as long as I have known Jim, I haven't danced with him. I really couldn't tell you even now whether he's good or not although at one time those things were vastly important to me. All I know is that the music is wonderful; that we manage to keep in step; that I am the proudest, happiest woman in that room or anywhere else.

"You smell awful good," I purr happily, rubbing my nose against his coat lapel.

"That's what they all tell me," he boasts. "It isn't my looks—it isn't my charm. It's always that heavenly smell of me that does them in."

"I wish," I say, "you would cease using the plural. It takes all the starch out of me."

"So you're going to be like that, eh? Well, we might as well take a firm stand now. I expect three nights out every week. . . ."

"Only three," I break in. "That's mighty handsome of you, pardner."

"And don't interrupt me. I haven't finished. I'm spending those nights out with—my best girl."

His arm tightens around me.

"Meaning me," I say blissfully.

"What do you think?"

The dance over we go into the bar downstairs, Jim insisting we toast the occasion with a champagne cocktail. He'd rather not use Sidney's.

We have clicked glasses and taken our first sip when one of the waiters from the Brand party approaches me and informs me that S. B. wants to see me.

It is with high good humor for once that I approach my boss. I am thinking it would be a nice gesture to make to let him know about our approaching nuptials. I have to tell someone or bust and it might as well be S. B., so I do not notice for the moment that his face looks like a thundercloud.

"Oh, Mr. Brand," I burst out. "We—Jim and I—are going to be married."

The boss takes this big. He looks at me, at Jim, then back again to me.

"I don't believe it," he says but there is no humor in his voice. Even in my condition I am aware he is being deliberately insulting. Instinctively I reach for Jim's hand.

"I'll admit it's difficult to believe," says Jim with a forced lightness, "but it's true."

"Things must be getting tough for you, Jim, if you have to really marry a girl."

I feel Jim stiffen.

"You wanted to see me about something, Mr. Brand?" I ask.

"I certainly do. When people work for me I expect them to give me their loyalty—their complete loyalty."

"What has that got to do with me?" I ask perplexed.

"Just this. I don't hire people to knife me in the back. . . ."

"Why don't you come to the point, Brand?" raps out Jim. "What's on your mind?"

"Who tipped off Anders that I wanted to get rid of him?"

"So what?" says Jim bristling. "You wouldn't have been celebrating here tonight if she hadn't."

"So—you admit it? When Anders told me, I couldn't believe him. He was feeling so good he thought he'd put in a word for Madge. I suppose it's the least he could do for her after she threw herself at him . . . and God knows what else . . ."

"Brand!" says Jim sharply. "I don't think you understand. Madge is going to be my wife."

I am only now acutely aware of the fact that we are the center of attraction and all eyes are turned on us. I see Selma pushing her way through the crowd toward us.

"For a naïve little girl," says Brand to me, "you do all right for yourself. Are you getting an affidavit from Bruce, Jim?"

Jim lunges forward. Selma screams. Brand's stooges whip behind Jim and hold him forcibly and a flashlight explodes!

When the atmosphere clears, Jim has been released and Mr. Brand is facing him with the thoughtful air of a man betrayed.

"To think, Jim," he philosophizes, "that you would try to strike me after everything I've done for you. I can't understand it. It's not like you."

"I don't approve of it myself," says Jim. "I was only going to show you how a hero really behaves. I've made you one so often I thought I'd demonstrate for future purposes—when I won't be there."

"I was coming to that," says S. B. sadly. "When I put my trust in people, I expect them not to misuse it. I trusted Madge—I trusted you, and you've both betrayed me. All my life I'm going to remember this and I hope that wherever you are and whatever you do, you'll remember that you let me down!"

I hear a voice—Stella Carsons's—cackle, "I think that's beautiful."

Love,
Maggie

MISS AGNES LAWRENCE   SEPTEMBER 4
KANSAS CITY MO

THINGS NOT AS BAD AS THEY APPEAR IN NEWSPAPERS
STOP ANYHOW HE IS GOING TO MARRY ME STOP HE
SENDS HIS LOVE STOP SO DO I

MADGE

THE GOSSIPEL TRUTH
Sidney Skolsky

September 4

The tender sentiments broadcast by a certain prominent producer in a Hollywood nightclub several nights ago, and swallowed whole by the colony, are a laugh. The victims involved, two of the swellest people I know, are now happily married in spite of it. Glad to have you back in the fold with us, Jim. How does it feel to make an honest living?

Silvia Schulman Lardner
Los Angeles, 1938